THE SORROWFUL STOWAWAY'S SALVATION

ELLA CORNISH

This is a work of fiction. Any names or characters, businesses or places, events or incidents, are fictitious. Any resemblance to actual persons, living or dead, or actual events is purely coincidental.

Copyright © 2022 by Ella Cornish

All rights reserved.

No part of this book may be reproduced in any form or by any electronic or mechanical means, including information storage and retrieval systems, without written permission from the author, except for the use of brief quotations in a book review.

Email: ellacornishauthor@gmail.com

CHAPTER 1

A horn blared loudly, announcing a ship's departure from the harbour, and promptly drowning out Joseph Tavers' genial but sonorous voice. Abruptly, he silenced himself, a small smile toying on his thin lips. The older man waited for the last notes to fade before returning his attention back to the young man at his side, beaming proudly as he pointed toward the water.

"Look there, Will," he announced, gesturing toward two still vessels in port, the cuffs of his pristine, white shirt showing beneath the sleeve of his navy suit jacket. "Those two beauties belong to our fleet."

William Tavers widened his intelligent, grey eyes, nodding admiringly at his father's announcement with respectful awe. Of course, he had known this piece of information. It was not the first occasion the boy had been required to view the ships which belonged to his family's trading company in his seventeen years. Many a time, he had joined his father on the docks or in the shipping warehouse, near the River Thames.

However, this time felt different to young William, the occasion special as Joseph was eager to show his son the inner workings of the business as William approached his graduation from Eton. It had always been assumed that the boy would take over the company upon his father's retirement even if the matter had not been openly discussed and William realised now that the time had come. He was eager to learn as much as he could absorb in the week before his return to school and he studied his surroundings with new eyes. He would not take over the business before he finished his apprenticeship, but every detail was of vast importance to the boy. He intended to absorb every morsel of information and make Joseph proud upon his return.

Vivid irises took in the sights with a new illumination, the dockworkers purposefully and busily striding past to direct and move cargo as it was unloaded from the ships, sailors loudly and boisterously congratulating one another on yet another successful turn at sea, their banter crass and cuss laden. The men immediately lowered their voices and hung their heads respectfully upon seeing Joseph at the dock, shuffling past to make their way to the local tavern to whet whatever of their appetites needed sating. Joseph Tavers was a man known in these parts and even if the sailors did not work for him directly, they admired the man on sight.

"Where is the Esmerelda?" William inquired, noting that a boat was amiss. He could not see her from where he stood and strained for a better look at the fleets around him.

"You have a good eye, boy," Joseph declared happily, clapping William jovially on the back. "You've been paying mind to our business after all."

He paused to cast William a wide, proud beam.

"She is halfway to the West Indies by now, I reckon. Or that is my hope, at least. Who can know with a journey so treacherous?"

William shuddered at the foreboding words. He could not imagine what dangers lay in the unknown waters beyond but reminded himself that the fleet had yet to be lost.

A shadow befell them, and a man cleared his throat politely, turning father and son away from the water.

"Forgive the intrusion, Mr. Tavers, sir."

A hefty man with a captain's cap appeared, bowing his head humbly next to Joseph. The Tavers men eyed him expectantly. In his hands, Captain Jonas held a thick wedge of papers for Joseph to oversee and Joseph reached for them.

"Very good, Jonas," Joseph said, accepting the outstretched pages before pivoting back toward his boy. "If you will, William?"

He moved closer to his father's side as Joseph focussed on the pages, nodding approvingly at the list of cargo. William swallowed a grimace, realising how little of it he truly understood.

"Is everything in order?" Joseph asked. William would have wagered that all was indeed in order, his father hiring only the most competent of men upon his fleets. Joseph's standards were high, and he paid better than most, ensuring that the crews took pride in their labours.

"Yes, Sir, Mr. Tavers. Twas a smooth journey from the America's. Nary a hitch 'cross the Atlantic from Alexandria."

"Very good."

With a final scan of the list, Joseph bobbed his head once more.

"You may unload now, Captain," Joseph conceded. William strained to read the small, even handwriting of the ship's log but with the sun quickly fading, even his young eyes had difficulty making out the cargo. Joseph shifted his shoulders back, permitting the boy a better view but William quickly found himself distracted by the unloading of goods from the ship.

This fleet was responsible for personal and business property, the clientele paying good sums for the proper handling of their wares from across the pond. To William's recollection, there had never been a complaint, the crewmen meticulous in the management of the cargo but his father was not apt to discuss business problems at their supper table.

I'll learn soon enough if there are issues, William thought, a fusion of excitement and nervousness plaguing him.

Massive steamer trunks marched past in the capable hands of the Ballantine's crew, never a frown nor grimace to be seen although William was quite sure they weighed tens of stones a piece. He pondered if he would ever be as strong as the men who worked for his father.

"Come along," Captain Jonas barked authoritatively, puffing out his chest. "There's no time for dawdling."

William saw no evidence of laziness, but he secretly admired the captain's commands and the way the sailors respected him.

Is he doing this for my father's approval, or does he always speak to the crew like this?

A gangly, skinny lad, with well-kept locks of dark hair, William never fancied himself much of a seaman. His feet were much sturdier on land, and he preferred them that way. He had been late to take to swimming, much to his father's hidden chagrin and the idea of spending his life at sea did not much appeal to the young man. Yet he could not deny a hint of envy as he watched the solid sailors filing past, single file, a crate or box between them.

Down the gangway, a commotion commenced, stirring the otherwise organised transport. At first, it was little more than a rumble of complaints but as the sailors neared, the words grew louder. Joseph whipped his head toward the activity, his verdant irises narrowing. Captain Jonas was first to react, his face waxing at the hint of an issue unfolding before the owner. It was clear he was not a man to accept embarrassment before his superiors and intended to nip the issue in the bud.

"What is the meaning of this?" the captain growled, striding deliberately towards the men, his eyes flashing with dismay. "What's the delay?"

A horrific odour wafted into William's nostrils and he gagged, turning away to smother his nose in a handkerchief, drawn from the breast of his jacket. Never had he smelt something quite so rancid.

"What is that repugnant stench?" Joseph demanded, his own complexion waning as he neared the men. "What is in that case?"

To William's disappointment, his father moved closer, leaving the boy little choice but to follow behind, much as he wished to sprint in the opposite direction. The scent grew more noxious as they neared, and William feared he might bring up the food he had for breakfast in front of everyone who watched. Yet there were no eyes on him.

"Please, sir," Captain Jonas begged of Joseph. "Stand back as I tend to this. There is no need for you to be sullied by a mistake."

"What is it?" Joseph demanded again, perplexed, making no move to back away. His dark eyebrows knit into a vee and William noted the green parlour of his jowls. It was little comfort to realise that his seasoned father was just as sickened by the reeking odour. "Have you improperly stored this case?"

The sailors looked uncomfortably toward one another, an uneasy but unspoken knowing shadowing their faces.

"No, sir. It was kept as it should have been," one man replied.

"What was meant to be in there?" Joseph asked, answering his own query with a glance at his notes. His frown deepened as he checked the labelling against his papers. "There should be nothing but household goods from what I read. Have they put meat in here?"

He sounded annoyed and disgusted by the notion and William again felt bile rise to his throat.

I must not vomit!

"The clients have been well-advised as to what can and cannot be brought across," Captain Jonas grumbled, clearly upset about the mishap. "Open it up at once. Whatever it is, we'll throw it out to sea. I'll deal personally with the offenders, sir. You needn't worry about that."

A crowbar was produced, one man prying the lid of the trunk to a splintered opening. The stench was unbearable now. Collectively, the men drew back, eyes widened in dismay, but the sailors seemed unsurprised by what they saw. William inched closer to get a better look, his head tipped sideways as he neared. Abruptly, a hand shot out, yanking him backward and the boy looked to his father, blinking. Joseph shook his greying head solemnly.

"No, Will. You do not want to see."

Confused, with his curiosity piqued, William almost forgot about the fetid smell but as he again attempted to look, his father's grip tightened over his arm.

"Oh Lordy," someone murmured, making the sign of the cross. The other men bowed their heads respectfully and a peculiar chill ran down William's neck and spine.

"Does he belong to you?" Joseph asked, his voice cracking slightly as he looked to Captain Jonas. William's eyes widened, understanding creeping upon him.

"Nay, Mr. Tavers. I don't believe he does," the captain answered grimly. "Although it's hard to say in his state."

Joseph inhaled a trembling breath. William had never seen his father so distraught.

"Get him out of there," Joseph instructed, pulling William back more. "Will, run now and find a constable."

"A constable?" William echoed dumbly. "What for?"

Yet he did not require a response. It was clear what had been found in the crate. A body of sorts.

But whose? And how does a body come to be in a crate?

A dozen useless questions flooded the boy's mind.

"You'll do as you're told," Joseph said gently but firmly, turning him away. There was no need for a copper. Matters on the sea would be handled amongst the crew, the laws of the water applying—even William knew such things. Yet Joseph clearly did not wish for his son to observe the atrocity they were about to unveil. He parted his lips to argue but the expression on his father's face made him reconsider.

William shuffled a few feet from the busyness but paused when he was certain his father was no longer watching. From where he stood now, the smell had diminished some, the fusion of seawater and dock rubbish commingling in his senses. He could not forget the terrible scent of decay however, not when he knew from where it had stemmed.

Who died and how?

Carefully but swiftly, the sailors reached into the crate and pulled a form from the depth. William gasped, his heart leaping to his throat as he realised the corpse belonged to a boy although Captain Jonas had been correct—the true nature of the body was difficult to determine with his blue-green skin, swollen and rotting.

"Good God!" someone choked out. "He's just a bairn!"

"Oh Mary, full of grace," another sailor mumbled, shaking his head, his fingers trembling as he crossed himself also.

"Whose is he?" Joseph's question boomed out as he looked to each of the men, anger lacing his tone. "Surely someone must know!"

Yet it was obvious they were all as stunned as William's father, none of them claiming the boy as their own.

"No one is missing from the roster," a sailor volunteered. "We're all present and accounted for, Mr. Tavers sir."

"He must have been a stowaway, sir," Captain Jonas announced, regaining his composure faster than his counterparts. "It isn't the first time this has occurred."

Dubiously, Joseph gaped.

"You oft come across teenaged corpses in boxes upon my ships?" he growled. "Surely that cannot be."

"Nay! No, sir! That is not what I meant!" Captain Jonas sputtered, his face paling more. "I merely meant to say that stowaways are quite commonplace. Tis the nature of the business, I'm afraid. Many attempt to flee the colonies for a better life and unfortunately perish in the process."

"How did he get inside the crate? Someone must have put him there!"

Joseph's eyes tore from one man to the next, but William could read no guilt amongst them. Stranger or not, the body was that of a boy and no one knew a thing about him.

William was certain he had never seen his father so upset in all his years. The older Tavers could not tear his eyes from the bluish flesh of the skinny frame and for a moment, he thought he saw water forming in Joseph's eyes. William forced himself to take in the boy, shock overtaking him as he fully understood the implication.

The corpse did not wear a sailor's uniform, confirming what Jonas had claimed about him being a stowaway. The boy's attire was nothing but a pair of soiled pants, his feet bare and filthy, covered in sores, much like the rest of his flesh which had not begun to decay.

Vomit filled William's mouth and he swallowed helplessly until he could no longer keep hold of his stomach. Retching into the water, he steadied himself against a post, knees shaking violently.

"Search the ship!" Captain Jonas commanded. "There may be others on board. Mr. Tavers is correct—the boy did not nail himself into the crate."

Through his peripheral vision, William watched the sailors scatter in all directions, eager to escape the dreadful scene on the dock and avoid Joseph's accusing eyes. Even the seasoned Captain Jonas appeared peaked and distraught, but he stood firm and attentive as he waited for his crew to return with news.

"Will!" His father was at his side before William could raise his weakened head. "Did I not tell you to go in search of a constable?"

"Forgive me, Father," he mumbled, despaired and sick. "I-I could not look away."

Joseph cast his son a sympathetic glance.

"Terrible business," he murmured. "He does not look much older than you."

"You don't imagine that someone put him in there over in the Americas?" William asked, dreading the answer.

"I should hope not!"

"How else would he have managed to find his way into the trunk?"

"You mustn't concern yourself with that now," Joseph told him, placing a strong hand on William's shoulder. "I'm aghast that you were forced to see it. I hope it will not haunt you, although the first corpse always will."

William wondered how many dead souls his father had been forced to behold.

"What will become of him now, Father?" Will asked softly. Joseph cast his eyes back toward the still body.

"I'll see that he has a good, Christian burial," he promised. "He deserves to be laid to rest in peace after the hellish journey he endured."

It was one of the many reasons William adored his father. For all his success and wealth, Joseph Tavers was a good, decent man who did not believe himself above any other. Many times, William had observed Joseph stop in the East End of London and offer coins to the urchin children who begged with their dirty faces and outstretched hands. He knew his father actively and regularly donated his time and money to the church, helping the less fortunate whenever he could. So often, the vicar preached to the flock about helping those in need and the richest of the city would nod in agreement but the moment the service finished, they turned a blind eye from those who desperately asked.

Joseph Tavers had always been different. Now, he was willing to foot the cost of a stranger's burial merely because it was the godly thing to do. A lesser man would have done as Captain Jonas suggested and thrown the boy into the river.

"Unhand me, ya beasts! I'll claw yer eyes out and feed 'em to tha pigs!"

The screams ricocheted across the waterway, pitching to a shrill and creating goosebumps on William's arms. The words as much as the tone curled his skin. He whirled around in time with his father, the pair gawping as a pair of sailors appeared with a girl flanked between them. William was shocked by the size of the child with her mouth as loud as it were.

"LEAVE ME BE!" she hollered. Her skin was covered in red splotches, filth covering her from head to toe. Her face was red and indignant through the soot of her face, her potato sack dress barely covering her scabbed knees. Like the dead boy, she wore no shoes, and her legs were covered in cuts and scrapes.

"We found another one, sir."

William stared in awe at the struggling child. She appeared no more than three or four, emaciated body ready to snap in half with her wild, flailing movements. The men seemed uneasy holding her, as if they, too, suspected she might break like a twig. She was undeniably malnourished, white paste forming at the corners of her mouth as they drew her down the gangway. It was impossible to determine the colour of her hair, but William suspected under the matted mud that caked her crown, there once may have been strands of fine gold although how he surmised such a thing, he could not say.

Furious blue eyes glowered at the men around her and her missing front teeth caused William to consider that perhaps she was older than he thought. She was in deplorable condition and the young man marvelled at the fact that she was standing at all. He reasoned that the sailors held the crux of her weight despite her violent struggling.

The child's gaze rested on William, her glare intensifying as he intuitively reached out a hand, despite the distance between them. He wanted to calm her down, to ease her terror that radiated beyond her fury. Like a trapped animal, he longed to release her but where would she go if he managed?

Joseph hurried back toward her, but William remained in place this time, watching as the child looked at the body at her feet. He was afraid of nearing her, afraid that she might somehow become like the boy in the box.

"Ya found him, did ya?" she announced, her accent distinctively American. William saw her bright eyes dim as they rested on the crate and then the bloated body on the dock. The wildness diminished if only slightly.

"Do you know him?" Joseph asked, his tone gentle. It was difficult to be cross with a girl so small and bewildered. She was clearly starved and likely ill.

God knows how long it's been since she's last eaten or taken water, William thought, appalled. If the boy's body had not traumatised him, the little girl was sure to do the job.

"He's ma brother," she growled, whipping her head away. "I only put him in there ta keep him from stinkin' to the high heavens. He warned me not ta get caught. Was the last thing he said, 'fore he kicked the bucket."

Her chin quivered but she did not shed a tear. William had not realised that he'd moved back into the circle of men surrounding the girl. He was just as enthralled with the feral, filthy creature as his father.

"Fetch her a blanket and water," Joseph called out suddenly, waving at a nearby crewman. They eyed him dubiously. "See if there's not something more appropriate for her to wear."

"She's a stowaway, Mr. Tavers," Captain Jonas growled. "I'll fetch a constable and have her detained."

"You'll do as I ask," Joseph insisted harshly. "She's at death's door herself and has lost her kin. I implore you to show the girl some compassion and forsake the idea of having a girl of four thrown in Coldbath to suffer abuses worse than you can ever imagine."

Captain Jonas appeared ashamed and snapped at his men, instructing them to do as Joseph commanded. The girl continued to use the last bit of her strength to fight them but her motions were futile against the scrappy sailors. She was simply too tiny.

"What are you called, child?" Joseph asked, kneeling before her. He did not mind that his fine clothing became dirty as they rested in a puddle. His hand extended to touch her face, but the girl gnashed her teeth and tried to bite him.

"Wouldn't ya like ta know!" she snarled like a feral beast. William swallowed a smile in spite of the situation.

"Yes, I would," Joseph agreed. "And the name of your brother as well."

She eyed him uncertainly clamping her thin mouth together.

"It's only proper that I know his name for his headstone," Joseph said patiently. "Else how will you know which grave is his when you wish to visit?"

Her small jaw slackened, and William caught a glimpse of a sea of rotten teeth.

She was ill cared for well before she came aboard the Ballentine, he realised sadly.

"Ya won't throw him out ta sea?" she demanded warily. "Ta be eaten by sharks and fish 'n crabs?"

Joseph shook his head.

"No. I'll have him properly put to rest in a proper grave. But I must know his name and yours, too, young miss."

She grunted rudely and finally stopped her struggle as if she recognised the futility of her actions.

"His name is Teddy."

"Theodore?"

"Teddy!" she yelled defiantly. "He ain't like bein' called Theodore. That's our papa's name and we ain't gonna be reminded of him none!"

"Teddy," Joseph conceded placatingly. "And you? What should we call you?"

"I..." she faltered and looked around desperately as if seeking her escape. Again, her eyes rested on William, and he also lowered himself to her level.

"You needn't be afraid," he told her softly. "You're safe now. We'll see you fed and watered and find you a fresh dress."

He cast his father a sidelong look, hoping his words were not an empty promise but Joseph nodded vehemently.

"Indeed."

One of the men returned with a blanket and draped it over the girl who nearly jumped out of her skin at the touch. She hissed and clung to the cloth, backing away as her captors released her. Only the dark water of the Thames stood behind her, a path forward blocked by the men. Horrified, William wondered if she might jump into the river.

"Please," William called out imploringly. "Don't run off. Nothing good can come of you roaming the streets of London alone in your condition."

He had little doubt she would not make it far. She stopped her backward walk, lips parting once more.

"London, ya say?"

"Indeed," Joseph replied. "This is London."

"We've left Virginia then."

Pity overwhelmed William. She was far too young to understand geography or the ways of the world.

Does she know that she's in another country, across the world?

"Yes, child. You've come to Her Majesty's Great Britain now," Joseph replied.

For the first time, the shadow of a smile touched her lips.

"Good!" she declared gleefully. Her chortle faded into a spasm of coughing and as another sailor attempted to thrust water at her from a distance, she stumbled forward to take it. Her steps were shaky, the fit growing worse as her rheumy eyes bulged.

"Father!" William cried, the Tavers rushing forward to catch her as she lunged forward awkwardly. The young man was able to embrace her before she could fall onto the dock, his own eyes widening at the feel of her skin. "She hot with fever, Father!"

The girl's eyes had closed and her breathing was shallow. Concern for her well-being engulfed William fully.

"Leave her here, Master William," Captain Jonas instructed. "I'll have her collected. She may be catching and she'll surely dirty your clothes."

"Nonsense," Joseph interjected, reaching for the limp child in his son's arms. "She'll come home with us, and I'll send for Dr. Wainwright forthwith. Come along, Will. There's no time to waste. The girl is in a poor state and will need care immediately."

The crewmen gaped at his suggestion, but Joseph's stare subdued them to silence.

"Arrange for the undertaker to come for Teddy's body," he instructed, spinning on his heel. He did not look back and William rushed to keep stride with him, ignoring the gawks of the men by the docks as he marched on with the rag doll girl in his grasp.

"Father, is this wise?" William whispered, shooting furtive glances about the harbour. "What if Captain Jonas is correct and she is infectious? Should we not find a hospital for her instead?"

"It is the right thing to do," Joseph answered unhesitatingly. "What is right and what is wise are not always one and the same, Will."

"I-I don't understand, Father."

"If we bring her to a hospital, it will only increase her chances of infection, if she does not have one already, or worsen one if she does. Her best odds for survival are away from others who are sickly, under Bessie's tender care. Moreover, the crown may claim her for being a stowaway. This is the best thing for her."

William did not argue with his logic but as they made their way to their waiting carriage, he found himself wondering what would become of the girl if she were to survive. He hoped that she would wake but he did not have high hopes for her. After weeks on the water without proper food or water, her chances were not good. Yet William could not forget her fighting, snapping spirit on the dock. He prayed that she would wake up and that he would eventually learn her name.

CHAPTER 2

The girl did not regain consciousness by the time the Tavers men returned to their grand house in Westminster. The estate had been in the Tavers family for three generations but maintained itself well under Joseph's constant supervision. Ivy climbed the stuccoed walls leading to the second storey balconies, twining along the eaves toward the triple chimneys on the slate roof. The interior boasted a fireplace in every room and woodstoves to warm the coldest nights.

William wished the girl would open her eyes to take note of their beautiful grounds. He imagined her eyes widening at the luxury he was certain she had never experienced in her young life. But she remained still, too still for his liking. Joseph dismissed their coachman who offered to carry the sickly girl into the house, tenderly wrapping her in his own arms and ascending the steps with William in tow.

"Have Rodgers send for Dr. Wainwright at once," Joseph instructed his son. William was reluctant to leave the guest room which had no linens or firewood, but he had little choice but to obey his father's instructions.

He nearly collided with Bessie in the hall, the servant's eyes shadowed with understandable confusion.

"What's happened?" she asked worriedly. "Why the need for the doctor?"

William barely knew how to explain what had occurred but managed to utter a few words on his way to summon Rodgers.

"There was a stowaway aboard the Ballentine," William explained, brushing past her. "A little girl and her dead brother. Father has brought the girl here but she's in a poor condition."

"Oh Lordie," Bessie breathed, sympathy colouring her plump cheeks, dark eyes clouding with sorrow. "I shall pray for them both."

William managed a wan smile for the woman. She had been with the family since William had been a boy, long before he had been sent to Eton for his education. In the aftermath of his mother's passing, Bessie had filled the role to the best of her ability, acting as governess, maid, and cook. William thought her more a guardian than a servant. He had often envisioned her marrying Joseph and becoming his mother in name.

"That would be lovely, Bessie."

"Are you well, Master William? You're quite pale."

"I'm fine, Bessie," he assured her. "I must send for the physician."

With a backward glance to him, the woman moved toward the room, pausing by the cupboard to fetch clean linens and William continued his way down the stairs to find the coachman. In minutes he had given Rodgers the instructions and the man promptly rushed off to find the doctor. William retreated into the house but as he climbed the stairs again, he heard Bessie and his father speaking in hushed tones.

"We must prepare for the worst," Joseph murmured. "She is in a very bad way."

William paused in the corridor, realising that his father did not wish for him to hear. "Her fever is high, and I suspect she has not eaten, nor has she drunk fresh clean water in weeks."

"She's quite small," Bessie whispered. "And covered in bruises. I daresay she's had a rough go at life already. How old do you reckon she is?"

"Initially I thought her three or four, but I wager she is closer to six, despite her size."

"Lord knows what would inspire two children to leave their homes behind in such extreme circumstances," Joseph murmured, his words cracking at the mere thought of what the girl must have endured.

"What is she called?"

"She never did tell us." Joseph sighed and William swallowed a small lump that had formed in his throat. Perhaps it was the closeness in age between himself and the dead boy or the mere sight of someone as frail and young as the girl so close to death. Whatever the cause, William was fraught with emotions he had never known before. His own mother had passed before the boy was old enough to truly remember her and while disease and apoplexy had claimed acquaintances in the past, William had never been quite so close to death before.

"She won't die," he declared, entering the room with confidence. Bessie and his father looked up in surprise. "She's far too scrappy. Did you see her at the docks, Father? Her time is not finished on this earth."

Bessie offered him a sympathetic gaze and busied herself with the linens, propping the girl's head against pillows and wiping her sallow complexion with a damp cloth.

"All we can do now is pray," she breathed. "God is merciful."

"We'll see what insight Dr. Wainwright will offer on the matter," Joseph said but William did not hear much hope in his voice.

∽

Dr. Wainwright suspected the girl was ill with an ague of unknown origin or perhaps cholera, an unsurprising diagnosis considering her weeks aboard the Ballentine.

"She must be transported to a hospital for quarantine," the surgeon ordered. "Her only hope is hydration and isolation."

"She'll remain here," Joseph intoned flatly, his words leaving no room for argument. The doctor adjusted his wire-rimmed spectacles and frowned but he did not protest as he secured his bag and straightened his form.

"I advise against it, Mr. Tavers but if you are insistent—"

"I am," Joseph interjected. Dr. Wainwright sighed a second time.

"See her hydrated and keep your distance," he instructed. "I'd not like to make this visit again for you or Master William."

"You needn't fret about us," Joseph replied, seeing the physician from the house, leaving William lingering in the doorway of the bedroom. Their voices drifted away and William ensured that they were out of view before retreating to the girl's bedside. He stared down at her, taking in the pale skin and matted, dirty hair. Bessie would be sure to bathe her now that the doctor was gone and he was curious to know if he were right about her hair colour. He leaned closer, searching for any sign of the blonde tresses he was certain hid below.

"You should wake now," he told her softly. "There's no one here but me and I'm not so scary, you'll see."

To his utter disbelief, her lids began to flutter and suddenly, he stared into a pair of blank, blue eyes. He gasped, falling back slightly, awed that his gentle chatter had worked to rouse her.

"You're awake!" he breathed, eyes darting back toward the door. He wondered if he should call out for Dr. Wainwright but stopped himself. There was little the doctor could do that he could not do himself.

"I'll fetch you some water," he told her. "Lie still."

Quickly he rose from his perched position to pour from the pitcher near the basin. The girl began to cough and sputter as William returned to her side.

"Drink," he urged her. She tried to refuse but her weakness made another fight impossible.

"Please," he implored her. "It is the only way to ensure you recover. I'll not have you faint again."

With shaking hands, she took the glass and pressed it to her lips, swallowing in deep glugs. The effort proved to be too much and her small head flopped back against the pillows, water spilling over the bedding as she did. William collected the glass and set it on the bedside table.

"You must drink and rest," he explained but she turned her head away to look toward the window. "It's what the doctor said."

She turned to stare at him as though she did not understand a word he spoke. William inhaled.

"Will you tell me your name now?"

She said nothing, an odd expression overtaking her face.

She does speak English. I've heard her myself. Why does she merely gaze at me like that?

"I am William Tavers. My father, Joseph, owns the ship on which you arrived in Great Britain," he went on. Her eyes shifted warily back toward him. "You met us at the docks. Do you remember?"

The girl remained silent, but William was beginning to suspect that perhaps she had little memory of how she had come to be there.

"Please," he begged. "Tell me what we can call you. I'd like to have a name for you."

"Ma brother," she rasped, moving to sit up, the memory striking her abruptly.

"He's being tended to," William reassured her. "As my father promised. He'll have a proper burial. You'll have an opportunity to visit the site—once you're well enough."

The child clamped her mouth closed again and William read the sadness lurking inside her. Her gaze darted about the room, taking in her surroundings with veiled awe. William wondered if she had ever been in such a house before, but he doubted it very much. Every inch of her visible skin was battered, bruised and scraped. This was not a girl of noble birth.

"You'll be cared for here," he vowed. "This is our home, and no harm will come to you."

"Master William!" Bessie appeared at the doorway. "Come away from the girl. Dr. Wainwright suggested that she might be catching."

William thought to argue but he realised that he could not afford to risk illness, not when he was coming to the end of his time at Eton. Following this, he would be joining his cousin, Richard, in Camden Town where he would broaden his understanding of economics. An illness would put a damper on any such plans. Yet William was far too intrigued with this little, fighting soul to leave without answers. He found himself less concerned with his own health than hers.

"I cannot force you to tell me your name," he said and sighed, rising. "Although I would very much like to know. Perhaps you can tell me your surname, one we can put upon Teddy's headstone."

The girl's head again whipped toward him, her eyes widening.

"Ya didn't lie about that?" she demanded, her words cracking with the effort of speaking. "Ya'll get him a headstone?"

"Of course," William replied, frowning. It troubled him to think a girl so young could already find the world so cold and suspicious. "You'll find we're honest folk, little miss. We mean precisely what we say and do as we promise."

She pressed her waxen lips together as Bessie ushered him toward the door.

"Please, Master William," she begged. "Your father will never forgive me if anything becomes of you. I would not like to tend to two sickly children."

William opened his mouth to argue that he was no longer a child when the girl cried out.

"Sarah!"

The pair paused and strained to look at the child who was struggling to sit against the bedding.

"Pardon me?" William said slowly.

"Ma name's Sarah…Joyce. Ya put Joyce on that stone, ya hear? Teddy Joyce. No Theodore."

William smiled and nodded, a small sense of victory flashing through him.

"Yes," he agreed. "I hear you, Miss Sarah Joyce. Rest now. I'll be by again."

"Nay, you won't," Bessie muttered, shooing him into the hallway and casting him a warning look. "You'll leave her in my care until Dr. Wainwright says otherwise."

William begrudgingly agreed but as he shuffled away, he knew he would not keep his distance. His curiosity was fully piqued about Sarah Joyce and how she had come to be an ocean away from her own home. Yet for now, he was content with having a name.

Over the next few days, William managed to sneak into Sarah's room with small treats and gifts to win her over. He wanted the girl to see him as a friend, not a threat and he hoped his small presents would prove his good intentions.

Day by day, she grew stronger, her pallor brightening. William found his guess about her hair had been accurate, the frail strands a stunning gold that rivalled the sun after Bessie scrubbed her down with lye and sweet-smelling oil. The bruising healed, the cuts scabbed over, and the child began to resemble a proper person by the week's end. While Sarah was far from fully healthy, she could now walk a few steps without falling but never ventured past the bedroom door.

Yet she spoke very little, ignoring William's offerings as he piled them against the bedside table, though her vivid eyes looked at the pink, satin ribbon with interest.

"You must give her time," Joseph told his son one day, catching the boy sneaking out of the bedroom where he had left a small piece of chocolate. "She has absorbed quite a shock for someone so young and she will not readily trust strangers."

"I realise that," William replied although he secretly wished to move her healing along. "I'm merely interested in hearing about her life in the America's. I will not force anything from her that she does not wish to share."

Joseph sighed and shook his head, averting his eyes from his son.

"I fear you do not," he answered, surprising William.

"Of course, I do," William insisted. "Oh, the tales she must have of the colonies!"

Joseph frowned deeply.

"Sarah has spoken to Bessie regarding some of her life in Virginia and it is not a tale for the faint of heart."

William stared at his father, willing him to elaborate but Joseph appeared reluctant to do so. He willed himself not to feel envy over the fact that Sarah had spoken to Bessie over him.

"Please, Father. I've come to feel a level of protectiveness for her," he implored. "I would like to know from where she's come and what has brought her here."

Joseph was swayed by his son's request and hung his greying head solemnly.

"If I tell you some of it, you cannot unhear it, Will."

"I would not like to unhear it," William said stubbornly. "Surely I have some right to know about the girl who lives in our home."

Joseph considered his words and exhaled in a long, slow breath.

"Like you, she lost her mother before she could recall," he began, shifting his gaze away. "But that is where the similarities end, I'm afraid."

"How so, Father?"

"She and her brother were left in the care of her father, a man who was not a kind soul. Teddy did his best to shield Sarah from their father's bilking and drunken ways but when the man began to turn his fists on the girl, her brother determined their only recourse was to escape. He did not know where the Ballentine was bound for, but it was the first ship he saw at the port and took it."

Appalled, William gaped. He had always known that his life was charmed but hearing the abuses bestowed upon a child so small chilled his very core.

"What kind of a brute puts his hands upon children?" he demanded, infuriated at his inability to seek justice for Sarah. Joseph shook his head sadly.

"Unfortunately, it occurs more than you think among the lower classes." He sighed. "I only tell you this so that you exercise patience and restraint with Sarah. She will come around at her own pace, but you must not force the matter. She has very little trust in others."

"Rightfully so!"

"Indeed."

William took his father's warning to heart but that night, as he sat by the fireplace in the parlour, reading aloud to his father from his favourite book, a moving shadow caught his purview.

Glancing toward the threshold of the room, he recognised the pale face peeking out from the corner and parted his lips to call out to the child, excitement clouding his good sense.

"Continue," Joseph interjected sharply before he could speak to Sarah. William darted a look toward his father and saw his warning expression.

Leave her be, his eyes seemed to say, and William recalled their conversation earlier. Clearing his throat, he continued before he could scare the child back into her room.

"When I speak of home, I speak of the place where in default of a better—those I love are gathered together; and if that place where a gypsy's tent, or a barn, I should call it by the same good name notwithstanding," he went on, noting that Sarah remained in the hall listening to his recount.

He considered it a small victory, even if she did not venture further than the doorway. Tonight, she lingered at threshold but who knew what tomorrow might bring? Perhaps Sarah Joyce would come around after all.

CHAPTER 3

Sarah made her ghost-like appearance every night provided William read aloud. The young man made a point to do so, even if his father was not around. He constrained himself from calling out to her, summoning her forward but through the small glimpses he took, he noted that she had begun to wear the ribbon he had brought her, twining it loosely in her golden locks. The shiny pink fabric shone brightly against her flaxen halo, a sharp contrast to the darkness in which she lurked. William wondered if she wanted to be seen but he did not question her presence, not once.

The night before William was due to return to school, he sat at the dining room table, waiting for his father to join them as they prepared for their final meal together. The notion of returning to school at such a time was bittersweet. William had always enjoyed his education and took pride in academics, but he could not deny that he longed to see what would become of Sarah in the coming weeks. He recognised that she was in good hands with Joseph, but he suspected that he would miss her dearly, despite only knowing her a short time. But for the few minutes a night she spent listening to him reading, she took all her meals in the room upstairs, isolated and silent.

"Where is Father?" William asked Bessie, eyeing the grandfather clock which ticked monotonously in the corner. It was unlike Joseph to keep his son waiting, even during his busiest moments. They had always made a point of eating together, a task which Joseph took great pride in keeping. Bessie turned her head away, but William caught the wisp of a smile upon her face. Amused and intrigued, he leaned forward.

"What is it? What do you know?" he demanded teasingly, reading her mischievous expression.

"I haven't the foggiest notion what you mean," she fibbed, turning away again to feign busyness. Footfalls prevented William from pressing the servant on the matter more and to his utter amazement, Sarah entered the dining room, Joseph immediately behind.

The girl was dressed in a lacy dress of white, her brittle, blonde strands pinned back to reveal her gaunt cheeks, but the boy noted that she had gained a small amount of weight. William stood, beaming as they entered but caught sight of his father's warning look, prompting him to avert his eyes.

"Good evening," he demurred, bowing his head. "Lovely to see you up and about, Miss Sarah."

She shifted her weight nervously and looked to Joseph who nodded encouragingly toward one of the high-backed chairs. For a moment, William thought she might turn and flee back up the stairs but with his father's bright smile, Sarah appeared to relax, if only slightly.

"This way, Miss Sarah," Bessie announced, pulling back on a chair for her. Sarah purposefully skipped her eyes over William and rested her gaze on the servant, hurrying to take her seat.

It was then that William saw she still wore the ribbon, cinched at the bottom of her frail braid in a bow. The sight gave him pleasure and it took every fibre of his being not to comment on the keepsake.

Dinner began to arrive on the table and Joseph deliberately ignored Sarah, silently encouraging William to do the same. The young man was awed by his father's ability to draw her out of her room, and he longed to ask how he had managed such a feat.

He did not and instead, they discussed William's impending return to school and plans for the future with his cousin, Richard. Several times, he witnessed Sarah cocking her head to the side like a confused pup as if trying to comprehend the technical terms used between the men but when William met her eyes, she blushed and looked away.

There is a little mind working furiously in there, he thought with bemusement. *Imagine what a fine education could do for her.*

"I daresay I was concerned that it would grow quiet with you gone," Joseph confessed, "what with your education keeping you away for longer, but now, perhaps, I'll have something to occupy my time in your absence. I always did hope for a sibling for you, Will."

He cast Sarah an affectionate glance and William swallowed his surprise. He had wondered what his father's intentions had been with the girl after she had recovered and now it seemed Joseph had announced them.

"Bessie," Joseph called to the maid who hovered nearby. "Would you be so kind as to bring forth that lovely apple pie I saw in the kitchen?"

Sarah's eyes were larger than the plates at the mention of dessert.

"I have it on good authority that someone here quite likes apple." Joseph made a pensive face and glanced at William. "Was it you, Will? Are you the one who so enjoys apple pie with fresh cream?"

William was instantly in on the ruse. He frowned and tapped his chin, shaking his head.

"While I do appreciate the taste of apple, I would much prefer plum or cherry. Bessie, have we any plum pie? I daresay, I would prefer it to apple."

Sarah's disappointment was palpable, and shame swept through William as he realised she took their banter seriously. Tears tickled the corners of her eyes and William immediately parted his lips to backtrack his comment.

"I'm afraid I have only apple," Bessie replied, glancing at the girl. "Moreover, I made it specially for Miss Sarah."

Relief coloured the child's face and Joseph nodded.

"That will do nicely as I remember now. It is Sarah who enjoys apple pie," Joseph announced. "Do ensure you bring a plate for yourself, Bessie."

The maid flushed and looked down, offering a small curtsey.

"Thank you, Mr. Tavers."

She hurried into the kitchen before Joseph could remind her that she was always welcome at their table. It was a bone of contention between Joseph and his peers. They did not like to be reminded that the servants were also people with souls as real as the wealthy. Yet Joseph paid their gossip no mind. His heart was pure and he would not be shamed into mistreating his house staff anymore than he would his own family. To Joseph's mind, there was no difference.

The servant returned a few minutes later, balancing four plates with expertise. She laid one before Sarah after serving the men and the girl attacked the dish with all the decorum of a feral cat. William could not help but gawk at her until Joseph nudged him gently underneath the table, forcing the boy to avert his eyes. He had not meant to stare but Sarah was unlike anyone he had ever met before.

"Bessie," Joseph called out pleasantly. The maid jumped to her feet guiltily, hastily wiping at the corners of her mouth where pie crumbs remained.

"If you've finished your dessert, would you be so kind as to play something for us on the piano? I've heard you practising when you don't think anyone is listening."

Bessie's blush deepened and her eyes popped.

"You've heard me?" she gasped.

"On occasion," Joseph replied, smiling. "Am I being too bold in my request?"

"No! No, sir. It would be my pleasure to play something for you."

William watched as she made her way toward the piano that had once belonged to his mother. Although the young man did not recall, Joseph often spoke of his mother Emily's ability to play. Joseph boasted that his late wife had been invited to play for the Duke of Hardingham before they were married. William suspected that his father thought tenderly of his mother when he permitted Bessie the freedom to play. Certainly, neither of the Tavers men had any aptitude toward the piano.

Bessie wriggled her fingers and slip onto the bench as William placed his fork on his now empty plate. Joseph sat forward, his arm resting on the edge of the mahogany dining table. Only Sarah continued to eat, oblivious to anything but the crumbs on her plate which she licked with her open tongue. Joseph paid no mind to her vulgarity and William stopped himself from reprimanding her.

She doesn't know any better. I mustn't embarrass her.

Yet it was difficult for William to tear his eyes from the girl as she sloppily lapped at the dish as if she were a dog.

That was, until the moment Bessie placed her fingers on the piano keys and sweet, melancholy music filled the dining room. Sarah's head jerked up, her eyes widening in shock. Bessie's tune began, a sad, high song that William had never heard previously. The music struck a chord in his heart but before he was granted a moment to fully feel it, Sarah leapt from her chair and rushed to the piano bench, squealing in delight. Rudely, she began to bang against the keys, a horrible, twanging noise flooding William's ears, ending the tune before it had truly begun. Bessie chuckled and William saw his father beam wildly, neither of them perturbed in the least by Sarah's bad-mannered interruption.

"I daresay the girl has a knack for music," he chortled, nodding encouragingly at Sarah. She paid him no mind and continued to slam on the keys.

"Aren't you bothered at the way she bangs on Mother's piano?" William cried out over the sound. Joseph shook his head, his smile broadening.

"I reckon that Emily would have found this very endearing," he replied. "This is how a family should sound. It is not always lovely music, Will, but it is everyone playing along together."

William could not help but chuckle, Sarah's naked happiness infectious. It was lovely to see the girl smile, and he was sad he would not be around long enough to see more of it.

CHAPTER 4

William crept through the front door as silently as he could manage, his bags in both hands. A waft of cooking meat met his nostrils, bringing a small smile to his face and he secured the heavy, oak door behind him with his boot.

Setting down his trunks, the young man paused to take in the grand hallway of his family home as if seeing it for the first time. In some small way, he felt as though it were new to him, his light grey irises taking in the familiar furnishings as a man, not a boy. Although he had visited several times over the past six years, this was the first that he would not be required to leave for Camden Town after a short stay following Christmas or Easter. He truly was home where he belonged and this time he was here to stay.

"Will!" Joseph appeared suddenly, his eyes shining with happiness to see his son. "You snuck in here like a fox! Have you no shame on an old man's heart?"

William chuckled and allowed his father to embrace him, returning the affection with as much vigour.

"I'd hoped to surprise you," he confessed. "Alas, you're much too astute for such antics."

"I know every sound of this house!" Joseph laughed, pulling back to study his son's handsome face. "My, how you've matured. Every time I see you, you're more a man than the time before."

His face brimmed with pride and William stood straighter, relishing in his father's affections.

"Master William!'

Bessie hurried from the back of the house, wiping her hands on her apron, dark eyes alight. On her heels, a properly dressed young lady followed, the hem of her dress sweeping at her ankles. William's brow raised to see the pair.

"Hello, Bessie," William called as they came to a halt, his eyes fixed on the girl. "And would that be little Sarah Joyce? It could not be! That girl had mud in her hair and only skin on her bones!"

Sarah smiled demurely but her eyes brightened to see him, curtseying with her hands folded in front of her. William was amazed to see the transformation in the child. At age eleven, she had become a true lady, any hint of the feral creature, wrestled from the docks forsaken.

"You only just saw me at Christmas," Sarah reminded him with a light laugh. "I haven't had mud in my hair for many a year."

"And yet you've grown more in that short time. I would not recognise you should I have encountered you on the avenue."

Sarah giggled again and looked away as William winked at Bessie. The servant's beam was as broad as his father's.

"Come in, Will," Joseph urged. "Rodgers will see your bags brought upstairs."

"You needn't trouble him, Father," William insisted. "I am fully capable of handling them myself."

"As you wish." Joseph did not argue, the joy in his tone unmistakable.

He's pleased I have not forsaken my upbringing whilst in Camden Town, he thought, picking up his trunks to march toward the second floor.

"Supper will soon be served," Bessie announced as William ascended the stairs to his bedroom. "Do not dawdle."

"I'll be along in a moment," he promised, noting Sarah watching him in his peripheral vision. He paused to look back at her. "Would you care to keep me entertained, Miss Sarah? I could gladly use the company as I unpack. I find it quite boring alone with my own thoughts for too long."

The child's face lit up and she nodded vigorously.

"Yes, please," she agreed, rushing up the stairs behind him. William swallowed a smile, realising that in some ways, the girl would always be the same. A child reared in the upper classes would do better to hide her excitement but for all of Sarah's finery, she was unable to contain her true emotions.

"Come along then." He continued to make his way toward his chambers, Sarah in tow.

"Have you truly come home to stay then?" Sarah quipped the moment they crossed the threshold to his room. "You'll not leave again?"

Any trace of her American accent had dissipated over the years, her education and training showing fully in her speech. She was truly becoming a proper lady.

Father ought to run a finishing school, William mused, impressed.

"I've no intention of leaving again," he reassured her, offering the girl a wink and smile. "Unless, perhaps, I take a wife in some exotic land."

Sarah's mouth gaped, her complexion waning at his words.

"Have you found a wife?"

William hooted with laughed and tickled the child beneath her chin.

"No, my dear. I've been far too occupied with my work to consider any such thing. You'd be appalled by the hours I keep. There's nary time for sleep, let alone a courtship."

Sarah appeared relieved.

"Would it be so terrible to have Father all to yourself?" he teased, turning his attention back to his trunks. He unpacked his suits and hats, hanging them in the wardrobe as Sarah perched at the end of his bed, her small hand draped over the post, watching him intently.

"I've had Father to myself," she reminded him, "however, I would like to see more of you."

William glanced over his shoulder and grinned.

"I'll ask your sentiments again after a month or two," he joked. "You may find yourself bored with me by then and calling out to the matchmaker."

"Never!" Sarah insisted. Her words filled William's heart with warmth. He had missed the girl as much as she had apparently missed him. Watching her transformation had been a source of secret pride in the young man, even though he realised he had little to do with it. Proper schooling, Bessie's tender care, and Joseph's doting attention had created a proper young lady out of Sarah, despite the odds that she had faced so early in life.

William was aware that his father wished to adopt the child as his own, but they did not rouse the subject with Sarah. Joseph feared that it would suggest an erosion of the bond she shared with her late brother, and he did not wish for her to forget from where she had come.

"We should return downstairs," William told her. "Lest Bessie returns with a wooden spoon for our hides."

Sarah's eyes bulged.

"Oh no!" she protested. "Bessie would never do such a thing."

She caught the mischievous twinkle in his eye and chuckled.

"You're jesting with me."

"I am," he agreed, extending his arm for her to take. Eagerly, Sarah accepted, and they retreated to the main floor. The scent of Joseph's pipe summoned them into the front room where they found the man sitting before the fireplace, puffing on his pipe, flipping through a periodical. He looked up as they entered, beaming proudly.

"This is a sight to behold," he announced, rising from his chair. "My children together after far too long. Come along now. Bessie has already cast me a stern look once. I would not like another for keeping her waiting."

"Bessie is incapable of stern looks," Sarah argued, and the men laughed.

"Indeed," Joseph agreed. "All the same, my belly is rumbling."

The trio entered the dining room, candlelight flickering across the stark white of the tablecloth and glinting against the silverware. Joseph pulled a chair for Sarah to sit before taking his own spot at the head of the table, William seated to his left. The younger Tavers could not stop smiling as he eyed Sarah, his admiration of her palpable.

"She's grown into quite a comely young lady, has she not?" Joseph commented, catching his son's expression. William chuckled.

"Soon she will be affianced with one of the sons of your associates, Father and we'll never see her at all."

Sarah blushed crimson.

"I will not!" she insisted, causing her family to laugh.

"Not until I return, I would hope," Joseph added offhandedly.

William's smile faltered and he glanced at his father, Sarah's head cocking with curiosity simultaneously.

"Return from where, Father?" William asked.

"Oh? Did I not mention?"

William's eyes narrowed slightly as he studied his father's face. Joseph deliberately turned away, hiding his eyes as he reached for a sip of wine.

"No, Father, you did not mention a trip," Sarah replied when William did not. "Where will you be going? Will I go with you?"

The older man cleared his throat and took a long drink before responding, causing William's eyebrows to shoot up further.

"Father?"

"Oh, all right," Joseph said and sighed with a hint of exasperation. "I'll leave in a week's time to investigate ports in the horn of Africa. And no, my dear Sarah. You will remain here."

William and Sarah gaped at him, the announcement clearly as much a shock to the girl as the young man.

"How long have you been planning this?" Sarah asked, stunned.

"It has been on my mind for a short while," Joseph said evasively. "I wanted to ensure that William had returned home, first."

"Where else would I have gone?" William said, dumbfounded.

"What will become of me?" Sarah demanded, her complexion opaque. Joseph raised his head and smiled warmly at the young girl, his gaze darting toward his son.

"I imagine that Will is apt to have his hands full over the next year," he replied. William's pulse quickened as he realised what his father implied. To be certain, Joseph confirmed his intentions aloud. "It is my hope that he will overtake the operations while I am away. I trust your training has aptly prepared you for such a task, son?"

Eagerness overcame William as he understood his father's question. He nodded vehemently, although he was disappointed to learn he would not have more time to spend with Joseph. He had long awaited the opportunity to prove himself worthy of running Tavers and Son Trading Co.

"It would be my honour and pleasure, Father," he assured the older man, his smile covering his cheeks in their entirety.

"More importantly, are you up for the challenge of caring for young Sarah?"

William and Sarah exchanged another glance, a fusion of uncertainty and excitement colouring their faces.

"I won't be a bother," Sarah promised hastily as though William pondered such a notion.

"I would hope not," he agreed, settling back in his chair. "I haven't the gumption to chase a girl your age about this house."

Sarah blinked but a small smile touched her lips as she again recognised that he was teasing her.

"It's settled then," Joseph announced as Bessie entered the dining room with dishes for the family meal. "William Tavers, I bequeath the throne to you."

They chuckled and reached for their respective cutlery, determined to relish and enjoy one another's company before Joseph made his way south.

It is bound to be an interesting year, William mused, and he looked forward to the challenge.

CHAPTER 5

The years that took Joseph away brought Sarah and William infinitely closer. It was nothing outwardly perceivable, no tangible event or force that occurred but their bond became unbreakable in a short time. The young man was impressed daily by not only Sarah's transformation but her quick mind and clever wit. Beneath her smooth, classy exterior was an impish girl whom William was happy to unleash whenever they were alone but in the public eye, there was no sign of the rebel child who had been dragged to shore that fateful day.

He often wondered if she worried that she would be abandoned or left to fend for herself if any glimpse of her former self was shown but he did his best to remind her that she was loved regardless of her past.

Perhaps she heard the whispers about town, the very same ones that William also heard, wondering about the orphan girl who had slipped so easily into the Tavers' lives. While Sarah never openly discussed the talk that she undoubtedly heard about herself, William knew it would be difficult for her to miss it.

William discussed the chatter with Bessie who scowled with anger.

"What a lot of old fudge," the servant muttered, dusting at the curio cabinet with stabbing force. "Busybodies and gossips with not a thing better to do than discuss the misfortunes of others. One would think that with all their good fortune, they would be apt to share it, not ridicule those without it."

William hesitated before posing the question weighing on his mind.

"Did Father ever think to send her away?" he blurted out. "To an orphanage?"

Bessie stopped abruptly, her lips gaping in shock.

"Not once!" she replied firmly, with a vehemence William believed. "Even in those early days, when Miss Sarah was as wild as a barn cat, it never crossed his mind. Mr. Tavers always knew that girl belonged here, with you."

Father is a good man. He would not want me to consider the flapping gums of nosy neighbours.

William fell easily into his role at Tavers and Son Trading Co. His years of training and education had prepared him well, but his father's tutelage had come in handy the most. He did not see himself as the owner of the company but as one of the men. He was as much captain as he was deckhand, secretary or servant. He understood his role and those of everyone else. The days of wobbly sea legs had passed, and he often joined the crew aboard their cargo vessels although he had yet to venture forth on a journey. The men respected him, and William proved himself to be a good employer.

At the end of the first year, a governess came to stay at the estate, enhancing Sarah's education as she attended an exclusive girls' school nearby. Yet their evenings were spent together, regardless of William's work or domestic commitments. Like his father, he recognised the importance of family and spending time together and he wished to instil those values upon Sarah.

"When will Father return?" Sarah asked one evening as they dined on a hearty meal of baked haddock and fresh, green beans. Bessie tinkled gently on the piano, her playing quiet as to not disrupt the soft conversation of the younger folk but loud enough for William to marvel at her talent. The servant had also thrived in his absence, her transformation visible in her playing. William had insisted she maintain her lessons and Bessie had in turn taught Sarah to play as well.

"I was saving the news as a surprise for dessert," he replied, wiping at the corners of his mouth and dropping the linen beside his plate. "But since you've asked, I cannot lie. I received a letter this morning. He's set to return any day."

Sarah's face brightened but she managed to keep her composure, nodding curtly as if the announcement had not filled her soul with the same joy that filled William's. Yet she had not mastered the art of stoicism entirely and William clearly read her glee.

"That is fine news indeed," she agreed, pursing her lips as if to keep from showing a toothy grin. At thirteen, she had begun to fill out her lacy gowns, her long hair gleaming and glorious against the puffed shoulders of her dress.

"I wonder if Father will recognise you," William teased. "When he left, you were a little girl. He may ask who has moved into his home in his absence and I will have a difficult time convincing him of who you are."

Sarah could not hide her grin now, her teeth showing now as she smiled.

"God does not care for fibbers, Mr. Tavers," she told him with mock reprimand.

"Who is fibbing?"

Bessie's piano playing faltered as the young people whipped their heads toward the doorway in unison. At the threshold stood Joseph, bedraggled and exhausted from his travels but donning a smile larger than any William had seen before.

"Father!" they chorused, rising from the table to embrace the man. Joseph extended his arms, allowing one of each to hold his children as they clung to his shockingly frail form.

"You've not been eating!" William chided him. Joseph laughed heartily, the sound turning into a cough. Hastily, he covered his mouth, untangling himself from the youngsters. When the spasm had passed, his smile returned.

"You'll understand the ways of the sea soon enough," he replied with a chuckle. "Life is more difficult on a ship than what you know here. There are occasions when dining is a luxury."

He coughed again and William frowned.

"Are you ill, Father?" he asked. Joseph snorted, ushering William back to his seat.

"Of course not," he scoffed, setting himself down as Bessie hovered nearby. He finally turned his attention to the housekeeper, his smile widening.

"Forgive my manners, Bessie. The journey has made me rude. How lovely to see you. I pray these hooligans have not given you too much trouble in my absence. I did write to you, but I fear any letters sent were lost in the travels."

"There was no trouble at all, Mr. Tavers," she replied, her face aglow. "Shall I fetch you a plate?"

"A glass of port would suffice," Joseph said. "I've no appetite for anything but discussion with my children at the moment."

"Very well, sir."

She hurried off to fill his order, leaving Joseph to study the pair.

"My, Sarah, you have grown into a fine, young lady! Have you a suitor I should know about?"

Sarah giggled and blushed, looking away.

"No, sir."

"Very good. I'd rather not have to clean my hunting guns," he jested. William snorted.

"That's for the best, Father. You're a terrible marksman," he reminded Joseph.

"That is a fact," Joseph agreed. "All the same, I would hope that Sarah and I have a few more good years together before she is married off and forsakes me entirely."

"That would never occur!" Sarah was aghast. Joseph opened his mouth to quip another response but again, a cough erupted over the table. Alarmed, William leaned toward him.

"Father, shall I send for Dr. Wainwright?"

"Hardly," Joseph sputtered, regaining himself. "This is what sea air does to a man's lungs. You'll find out yourself in a month or two, Will."

William's dark eyebrows rose in question.

"How's that, Father?"

"I've a journey in mind for you," he explained. A fusion of excitement and concern meshed in William's gut.

"Oh?"

"Whilst trading in Africa, I came to learn of some good investments. We must act quickly or risk losing the advantage."

William's stomach sank but he willed himself not to show his disappointment.

"Where to, Father?"

"To the West Indies, I propose. There's a voyage impending in six weeks and I would like to see you aboard."

William swallowed and forced a nod but before he was able to speak, Sarah yelled out.

"NO!"

Sarah's dismayed cry forced the men to peer at her. She shook her head vehemently. "You've only just returned! I'll not have Will leaving now!"

"And I shall remain," Joseph reminded her reassuringly, a twinge of confusion touching his face. Yet William understood the girl's upset. He reached across the table for her hand which she offered reluctantly.

"You mustn't worry, Sarah. Nothing untoward will occur. I'll return as quickly as Father did."

"Father was gone for almost two years!"

"Sarah…"

"You can't be certain that nothing will occur on the sea!" she fired back, withdrawing her palm to fold her arms under her chest. "Teddy would say differently—if he could."

Joseph inhaled sharply but William was not surprised. Although she did not often speak her brother's name, her anxiety of Joseph's trip had rested heavily on Sarah's slender shoulders for months.

"Those circumstances were quite different," William reminded her gently. "Our voyages are well supplied with good, competent men. I will return to you just as Joseph has."

He cast his father a sidelong look and Joseph nodded reassuringly.

"There is nothing to fear," he promised. Sarah swallowed her clear indignation, her eyes flashing with sorrow and anger.

"May I be excused?" she asked, her voice taut.

"Sarah, Father just—"

"Yes, my dear," Joseph interjected. "You may."

Sarah rose without another word, cerulean eyes averted as she slipped from the dining room. The ruffle of her hem faded away, leaving the men to stare after her.

"Has she been difficult the whole time?" Joseph asked. William's eyes widened and he shook his head.

"On the contrary. She has excelled in her studies and helps Bessie whenever possible. She's been doing very well. But she has missed you, Father."

"And I have missed you both terribly. Perhaps it is not a good idea to send you off so soon."

"It is not soon," William corrected him. "It's been years coming and I am more than ready to embark on such a journey. As you say, we must act quickly or lose the trade."

Joseph appeared relieved by his son's surety, his shoulders relaxing. Another small cough fell from his lips but before William could comment, he held up his hand.

"I am merely releasing the sea air," he chuckled. "You'll see. You'll endure the same fuss when you return from your own journey."

William nodded, closing his lips.

"Why don't you see to your sister?" Joseph suggested. "Assure her that this is all very commonplace and that she has little to fear."

The younger Tavers rose as Bessie returned to the dining room with his father's glass of port. He observed the small glance shared between employer and servant, his interest piqued by the expression, but he did not allow himself a moment to pursue it.

He immediately located Sarah in the library, who was peering out into the yard behind the property, staring blankly into the fields.

"I understand that books are more interesting than boring landscapes," he teased. "You might try to read one."

She did not look at him, her lower lip extended slightly. Sighing, William sat beside her at the window seat.

"I realise your concerns," he began.

"My brother died," Sarah reminded him. "As I almost did. I held my tongue when Father went but I was strained the entire time he was away. Now I must do the same again?"

"You needn't remind me about Teddy and you," William muttered. "It's not something I'm apt to ever forget."

Sarah's face softened and she pivoted her head to peer at him.

"Why must you go?" she demanded. "You've run matters so well here in Father's absence. Why must you leave?"

"It is part of the business, Sarah. I know you understand that."

She said nothing but William could clearly see the wheels turning inside her mind. As he had so many times before, he pondered what the old Sarah Joyce would have said. He reasoned he was happy not to know in this instance.

"I wish you didn't have to go."

"I will miss you too."

She struggled to produce a smile but failed. William took her hand and squeezed it softly.

"I'll write often," he vowed. "Every day."

The corners of her mouth twitched but she still did not smile.

"You'll be far too busy."

"I'll make time," he insisted, unsure if he were promising more than he could deliver. Yet he wanted to bring a smile to Sarah's face at any cost.

She sighed. "I'd much rather you promise your safe return."

"That I will," he swore. Sarah was not convinced, and William knew there was little he could say that would change her deep-seated insecurities, borne from the time before he had ever known her.

Was there ever a time that I did not know her?

William could barely recall such an era.

"Please, be vigilant, Will," Sarah begged, the plaintiveness in her voice cracking his heart some. "I would not know what to do without you."

"You will never have to know," he swore. "Now, come back to the table. Bessie mentioned something of apple pie for dessert."

He was not surprised to read the interest on Sarah's face, but she did not lose the shadow of doubt. She stood and nodded, an expression of sheepishness overtaking her lovely, bright eyes.

"Father must be disappointed in my response to his arrival," she murmured, blushing sheepishly.

"No," William corrected her. "Father is relieved to be home with us. I suggest we enjoy our time together."

While we have it, he added silently. He could not deny that his own heart cracked at the prospect of leaving when they had only just been reunited. William was determined to make the most of their moments, fleeting as they might be.

CHAPTER 6

The wind whipped wildly, knocking half the crewmen back as they struggled for control of the ship. Water sprayed over the sides of the boat, sucking into William's nose and forcing a drastic cough from him. Captain Baxter shouted out commands, but they were lost against the gale, rain pelting violently down.

"Mr. Tavers, sir, please! See yourself below deck!"

William could not hear nor see who it was that yelled out to him but a moment later, strong arms yanked him out of the monsoon toward the belly of the ship. The Esmerelda rocked, creaking and groaning, water spraying through newfound holes even in the faux safety of the underbelly. If the ship were to sink it would be far worse in the caverns of the vessel, but William did not fight to find his way back deck side. He trusted in the crew and captain who had undoubtedly experienced storms like this before, but it did not slow his racing pulse. The voyage had been cursed from the beginning, it seemed. The monsoon was merely another in a long line of catastrophes that had struck.

William fought his way back toward his bunk, shivers crawling down his spine at the memory of the pirates who had been narrowly thwarted weeks before and the hurricane that had damaged part of the ship.

Will we survive the latest?

He closed himself inside the cabin, goosebumps prickling his skin and he opened his steamer, digging for the thick wad of letters in their depth. It had been months since Sarah had last written but that was through no fault of her own. Their travels had taken them off their scheduled path and away from common ports where mail could be easily sent and received. A full beard now covered William's face and he ran his fingers nervously through the wiry hair as he reread Sarah's words.

Happy birthday, Will. I find it difficult to believe that you've been gone an entire year. It feels as though you have only just left yesterday, the pain in my heart still fresh. Father's condition is frail now, but he insists that it is merely a mark of old age. I fear that matters are worse than he allows me to believe but he refuses to allow me or Bessie to call on Dr. Wainwright...

He set the letter aside, dread and regret forming inside him. The letter was almost a year old now, his twenty-fifth birthday a few weeks away.

Assuming I make it to May, he thought grimly, the echo of agitated voices rifling through the walls of the cabin. Below him, the boat continued to rock mercilessly but the jarring motions seemed less than when the storm had struck. The captain was regaining control of the vessel, slowly, but the water continued to spray inside the holes at an alarming pace.

Will reached for another letter, eager to set his mind on something other than the chaos erupting around him. He was of little use to the crew, and he did not wish to get in their way but he could not merely sit still and pray for God's mercy.

His fingers curled around another envelope but as he pulled it from the trunk, the cries above him grew louder and his head jerked up.

"Batten down the hatches!" someone howled. "She's going down!"

"Whistle for the wind, men! The end is nigh!"

Each word sent a knife of terror but as he leapt to his feet, William was plunged forward, face smashing into the cabin's wall before him. The ship groaned again, the sound of splintering wood causing more fervent yells overhead.

William's life flashed before his eyes as the boat impacted something, screams echoing through his mind as the world went entirely black.

∞

Sarah inhaled a shuddering breath, her pale hands trembling as she placed them over Joseph's waxen cheeks. Each moment, he seemed weaker, sucking the life from Sarah's body along with his own.

"W-Will?" the man mumbled. "Will, is that you?"

The girl swallowed the lump in her throat, shaking her head.

"No, Father. It's me—Sarah."

Joseph blinked his rheumy eyes, struggling to focus on the girl.

"The Esmerelda," he muttered, barely coherent. "H-has it been found? Have they found Will?"

Tears blurred Sarah's vision but she managed to contain them, determined to remain strong for her guardian. He had been the pillar of strength for her during the worst times of her life. The least she could do was return the favour to him.

"You must rest, Father," she told him quietly. "You needn't worry yourself about business."

"Will is not business!" Joseph protested but his vehemence forced a fit of coughing from his lungs. Sarah winced at the sound, a commonplace noise in the Tavers' mansion but it did not make it any less daunting. There was no doubt about Joseph's fate now and with William lost at sea, Sarah recognised that she alone was responsible for seeing the man off to his afterlife.

Silently, she prayed to God for a miracle, a divine intervention which would bring her adopted father back to life, and William too.

If William were alive, he would have returned by now, she thought miserably. *And Joseph is not my adopted father. I never asked him to make me legally his kin.*

As if reading her thoughts, Joseph grabbed for her hand, his eyes widening.

"Send for the barrister," he wheezed, his eyes popping. "I'll see you adopted before I go—"

His speech was interrupted by a spasm of coughs, each one worse than the last. The sound exploded goosebumps over

Sarah's chilled skin. It seemed she had been unable to warm herself for weeks.

"Rest, Father," she begged him, swallowing her tears. "You must not concern yourself with anything but healing."

"Will," Joseph moaned. "Where has he gone? Sarah, send for Nigel Harris!"

Sarah was incapable of holding back the tears in her eyes and she abruptly rose from her spot at Joseph's bedside, hurrying out of the room, Bessie extending a hand toward her, a commiserating sound escaping the servant's lips.

"Miss Sarah…"

The tears flowed freely and fully as Sarah retreated to the study, slinking into her favourite spot near the window. So many days she had spent in that precise spot, by the window, peering into the world beyond. Yet she had never gone there to cry, her heart breaking with the grief of losing the only family she had ever known.

"Miss Sarah."

Hastily, the girl wiped at her eyes, turning toward the maid who hovered by the doorway, her own pain evident.

"Please, Bessie," Sarah rasped. "I need a moment."

"There isn't a moment, Miss," Bessie replied. Her response startled Sarah. It was unlike the servant to be contrary.

"What is it, Bessie?"

"You should go for the barrister at once," Bessie promptly explained. Sarah stared at her, stunned at such a callous instruction.

"Father is—" she could not bring herself to say the words. "My adoption is hardly paramount."

"But it ought be," Bessie urged. "Miss Sarah, you are all who remains, with Master William gone. When Mr. Tavers passes…"

She visibly gulped, her gentle eyes pooling with unshed tears of their own.

"I don't wish to speak of such things," Sarah interjected sharply, unwilling to hear Bessie's inevitable words. "We must pray for him."

"Miss Sarah," Bessie murmured. "Mr. Tavers is beyond prayer now. If you wish to hold any legal standing over his holdings, you must be his kin."

The words were a slap in the face to young Sarah. At fourteen, she had no sense of such technicalities but, inherently, she understood that Joseph's impending demise would surely create problems for her.

"Miss, I understand this is difficult for you, but you must think of your future. With Master William…there is no one but you to carry forth the Tavers' affairs. Please, think of what will become of you."

Sarah merely stared at the servant, shaking her head. Surely Joseph had made arrangements for her…had he not?

"It does no harm to bring the barrister in at Mr. Tavers' request," she urged when Sarah hesitated. "But you must not waste a moment. It may already be too late."

As Father does not have much longer.

"I'll send Rodgers at once," Bessie pressed, awaiting her approval. Conflicted, Sarah found herself nodding despite the wariness in her heart. It seemed disloyal, greedy to be thinking of such things under these circumstances. Yet she knew Bessie loved Joseph as much as the girl and would not suggest anything to dishonour him.

Without a word, Bessie hurried away to find the coachman, leaving Sarah to ponder what was next to come.

Please God, she begged. *Save us all.*

~

The finely dressed lady eyed the bearded stranger with naked contempt, her hand curled around the wood of the door. He craned his neck to look inside.

"Sir, you have the wrong address," she insisted for the third time. "There is no Joseph Tavers here. Please, be on your way or I'll have little choice but to call on a constable."

William gaped at the woman but he had little time for a reaction as the door closed in his face. Stepping back, he stared up at the house in which he had been born and raised, wondering if he had lost his wits at sea.

The shipwreck had stolen another six months from his life, prolonging his time abroad by more than two years. Although business had proven fruitful from a financial standpoint, William continuously wished he had not agreed to the journey across the Atlantic. It had been ill-fated from the moment of departure, the Esmerelda destroyed en-route. He had been forced to charter a much smaller vessel for the return passage to England with half the crew. The only modicum of sanity William maintained was through rereading the letters from Sarah and the hope that he would again see her and his father.

He raised his fist to again knock at the door, insistent on knowing what had become of his family. It had been five years since he had last set eyes on the house, but he knew he had not lost his wits, nor would his father readily sell the home which had been in their lineage for generations. Something was truly amiss.

"Please!" he called out when no one responded to his knocks. "I must know what's become of my father!"

The door remained ominously closed, leaving William little choice but to back away, shaking his long, unkempt head of hair.

Turning away, his eyes scanned the avenue, hoping for a familiar face. He considered knocking on a neighbour's door but abruptly had a better thought.

Surely, he must be at the shipping office, he realised, feeling foolish he had not considered it before. Sheepishly, he rushed off, embarrassed at his behaviour, and trekked toward the East End docks. He was bone weary, exhausted, and hungry but that did not slow his gait. He had waited for this moment for far too long to pause and rest at one of the taverns which beckoned him with as much allure as the ladies of the night who grinned salaciously.

William ignored them all, thinking only of Sarah.

I will not recognise her, he thought with growing excitement. Many a night, he had lain awake trying to imagine her as a young lady. The year he had spent with her had bonded a closeness between them that he was not apt to forsake. He hoped that she had not forgotten about him either.

The bustle of the docks met his ears, the familiar stench of salt and decay meeting his nose, but it did not faze William as he strode toward the warehouse. The sailors laughed, chattering loudly as they disembarked their latest hauls, dockworkers shuffling by with massive crates and steamers. William found himself staring after one, thinking of the afternoon that Sarah had come into their lives.

"Oy! Mr. Tavers!"

The sound of his name shattered William's reverie and he pivoted to see one of the crewmen striding toward him, his face pinched into a scowl.

"Lacey," William replied with a nod. "I'd have thought you would be home with your wife and boy by now."

"Not without me pay," the man replied with a growl. "What's become of your father's shop?"

William's brow furrowed and his head lifted toward the signage looming overhead. Blood drained from his face to realise that the Tavers and Son Trading Company no longer sat where it had always been.

"I-I—" William sputtered, his eyes widening at the sight.

"Where is your father?" Officer Lacey demanded. "I've a right to be paid! After what we've endured—"

"And you shall be," William interrupted, a stoic expression befalling his face. "Surely this is a miscommunication of sorts. Have you gone inside?"

"Yeah! Of course," Lacey barked, his manners leaving him at the thought of being jilted for pay. "It's a cannery now, yeah? They tell me that Tavers and Son has been shuttered."

Wind knocked out of William's lungs.

That's impossible! he thought, unable to hide his shock.

"You didn't know?" Lacey demanded suspiciously.

"I've not had contact with anyone in several years," William confessed. "But I've sent sums home along our travels."

His speech faltered some and he pondered a thought that had crossed his mind several times over the past two years. Not a single correspondence between himself and his father or Sarah had been answered since before the shipwreck which had left him stranded on a remote island for months. Even after finding his way to the West Indies, sending and receiving mail had been a notorious task.

But not a single word from either of them?

He paused and dug into the depth of his pockets, withdrawing a pouch.

"What's this then?" Lacey asked suspiciously, eyeing the bag with mild interest.

"This is not all you're entitled to, but it will keep you until I sort matters." William plopped the sac into Lacey's hands and marched forward, not permitting the officer to argue.

The odour of fish permeated the docks, following him long after he had left the Thames behind and headed inland toward the city. The streets were strange to him now although not a great deal had changed, and he found himself before the barrister's office with relative ease.

A young, harried-looking man sat among a flock of papers as William entered, barely acknowledging the newcomer.

"Pardon me," William said after a moment of being ignored.

"Yes? What is it?" the secretary demanded, his face pinched and flustered.

"I'm in search of Nigel Harris."

The overworked clerk finally raised his eyes, resting his gaze on William.

"He's not here," he replied flatly.

"When will he return? It's quite a matter of urgency."

The young man smirked slightly, his dark eyes raking over William's unkept appearance.

"He won't. He's dead."

William gasped, remembering the man who had been his father's attorney for as long as he could recall.

"That's terrible!" he choked. The legal assistant shrugged and resumed his affairs until William splayed his hands over the mound of files and forced his eyes back up again.

"He dealt with the care of my family's affairs for many years," William explained, striving to keep his voice even. "Who has since taken over his accounts?"

The clerk frowned, cocking his head as though weighing the validity of William's claim.

"Who might your family be?" he asked, not bothering to hide the sneer in his tone.

"Joseph Tavers is my father," William answered unable to keep the note of pride from his voice. "I am William."

"I'll see to this, Calvin."

A handsomely attired man emerged from a closed door, adjusting his spectacles.

"Forgive my man," he said pleasantly. "He hasn't an inkling, in most instances. My name is Adam Warmingham. I'm the barrister of record."

"You've taken over Mr. Harris' accounts?"

"Some," Mr. Warmingham replied. "How may I be of service?"

"My father—his business…" William trailed off for a moment, unsure of what to make of any of it. "I've been abroad for several years and come home to find my house occupied with strangers and my father's company no longer in place."

Mr. Warmingham's eyes grew larger.

"Who is your father?"

"Joseph Tavers of Tavers and Son Trading Company."

Mr. Warmingham shook his head, frowning slightly.

"Please, come inside," he urged, causing William's heart to flutter nervously.

"Do you know him?"

"I do not." Disappointment overtook his worry. "However, I will have Calvin locate any files pertaining to your father."

Mr. Warmingham nodded deliberately at Calvin who barely smothered a groan, but the barrister was already leading the way toward the open door of his back room. William followed the man inside the inner office, noting Calvin's exasperated expression but he did not much mind making the surly clerk work more.

"Allow me to fetch you a drink while Calvin seeks the information," he offered cordially. "I pray you will not take offence when I suggest that you look as though you could use a stiff whiskey."

William was not offended in the least. The thought of a full drink to calm his unsettled nerves more than appealed to him. Mr. Warmingham did not await a response, ambling toward the drink cart set off to the side of the room, shaking his head as he did.

"You claim you've been abroad for several years?" he offered by the way of conversation, his hands working to produce two glasses. "May I ask where you've been?"

"The West Indies," William replied. "My father owns a trading company and I was off to scout for a new route but was met with several misfortunes along the way."

"How harrowing."

Mr. Warmingham placed a glass of crystal in William's outstretched hands.

"And you haven't had contact with your father since your departure?"

"I stopped in port along the way but the further we sailed, the more tumultuous postage became," William explained, guilt flooding him.

Why did I not try harder? Why was I not alarmed?

A knock on the office door spared the men from more idle chitchat and Calvin appeared, a file in his hand.

"Have you located the Tavers' information?" Mr. Warmingham asked. Calvin nodded curtly, thrusting the folder forward before wordlessly disappearing back to his tasks.

"Again, you must forgive him. He's not much for social etiquette but he is quite a brilliant clerk."

William cared little for Calvin and his surliness. His only concern was what had become of his family. Mr. Warmingham took a seat, carefully opening the folder. His graceful, precise movements only fuelled William's anxiety and he wished the man would get on with it.

"Well?" he demanded impatiently. "What does it say?"

Mr. Warmingham lifted his elegant head, adjusting his spectacles as a small frown appeared on his lips.

"I am deeply regretful to inform you, Mr. Tavers but…it appears your father has passed on."

The words were a physical blow to William who sat forward in a lurch, his drink spilling before he was afforded the benefit of a single sip.

"Pardon me?"

"Forgive the blunt address," Mr. Warmingham offered sympathetically. "I fear there is no easy way to inform someone of such a tragedy."

"How? When?" William sputtered, disbelief clouding his vision.

"Three years ago, it appears. The records tell us little of how he came to pass."

Blood drained from William's face and he sank back, shaking his head.

"No…" he muttered. "It cannot be."

"There was no one to claim his affairs." Mr. Warmingham frowned, his eyes scanning the pages before him. "Tavers and Son Trading Company was closed, the ships sold at auction."

"Sarah!" William choked, eyes widening.

"I'm sorry?"

"My...Sarah Joyce. She was my father's ward for many years. What became of her? Of the house?"

Sighing, Mr. Warmingham replaced the file on the table and folded his hands neatly before him.

"Again, you must forgive my boldness, Mr. Tavers, but it appears as though the business was in dire straits prior to your father's illness. The house was behind in payments and foreclosed upon soon after Mr. Joseph Tavers died. I cannot speak as to this ward as there is no indication of her here."

"There must be!" William thundered, unable to accept all he had just learned. "A man of my father's bearing did not simply have his legacy, his ancestral home, wiped out in a matter of years!"

The barrister exhaled again, shaking his head.

"I am unsure of what to say, Mr. Tavers. I did not know your father personally as I explained, and Mr. Harris is also deceased. Perhaps Miss Joyce has gone to stay with relatives or friends."

William gaped at the attorney, his mind whirling.

Who would take her in? We were scorned upon for bringing her into our home from the start.

"Where would one go if they had nowhere to go?" he whispered, more to himself than Mr. Warmingham. Of course, the lawyer had no answer for him.

"I'm deeply sorry for your loss—your losses," the barrister offered as William rose to his feet. "If you find yourself in need of representation—"

Yet William heard none of the man's words, his feet carrying him towards the door and out into the lobby where Calvin remained working.

"Mr. Tavers!"

William stumbled out of the offices, his legs weakening with each step until he could no longer keep himself upright and he fell against the road. Horses' oncoming hooves did not move for him, his eyes trained blankly on the darkening sky overhead. Shame and confusion blanketed him, a thousand memories of his father crossing through his troubled mind in a torrent. He had failed Joseph as much as he had Sarah and now they were both lost to him forever.

Sarah, where are you? he called out silently. *Oh, God. What have I done?*

CHAPTER 7

Her hands worked tirelessly against the looms, ensuring that the spools did not twist or curl. After two years of working at the cotton mill on the outskirts of London, Sarah had long since learnt the tricks of the trade, her fingers working almost by rote.

The din was commonplace to her ears now, the horrific noise of machinery clunking in her head and creating a dull pounding that never quite diminished. Yet if Sarah had to choose the worst form of torture brought about by her employment, she would certainly claim it to be the incessant cloud of fibres that permeated the air and settled in her lungs.

Bessie spent the nights coughing after their twelve or fourteen-hour shifts, adding to the noise in Sarah's mind. It caused her distress to see the woman she had come to regard as a mother in such distress after a life of servitude.

She wished there was money to see a physician, but the prognosis would not help. They were two desolate souls, thrust into a world that neither one of them could have foreseen. So many evenings, Sarah laid awake on her lumpy, straw mattress in the East End of London, thinking of the night Joseph had passed, minutes from signing on her adoption. Nigel Harris had arrived too late, leaving Sarah with nothing in a span of minutes.

Yet the pain of losing her family was far greater than anything else to Sarah's mind. She had long since resigned herself to the fate of her life in the cotton mill, alongside her one friend in the world.

A horn blew, indicating their shift was complete and Sarah looked for Bessie. As she turned, someone shoved her roughly and Sarah frowned.

"Watch yer step, princess," Angela Yates hissed, pushing past the girl. "We ought not move fer ye in these parts."

Sarah grimaced at the woman, long accustomed to the abuse that Angela and the other women instilled upon her from the moment she and Bessie had arrived. Sarah's good manners and decent clothing annoyed the others in a way that the girl did not understand. They were all in the same situation, regardless of what had led them there, but Sarah's clear education irked her fellow workers beyond reason.

"Miss Sarah, shall we leave?"

The girl cringed at Bessie's address, realising that it did not help matters. Angela and her posse of hens clucked gleefully.

"Imagine. A cotton worker with 'er own servant," Gertrude Morrison chortled. "Where would I get me one of those?"

"Ye'd 'ave te be high born, ye fool," Angela sniggered. "I wonder what 'er papa did te put the princess in this situation, I'd rightly like te know."

"You'll sooner know my fist to your eye if you don't move along," Sarah hissed, advancing on the women. They scattered, smiles faltering as they recalled the first time the girl had laid a hand upon them. No one had suspected that the dainty, well-spoken blonde woman could pack such a punch.

"Miss Sarah, you must ignore them," Bessie muttered, ushering her toward the doors of the factory. She paused to permit herself an explosive cough, causing Sarah to forsake the cruel women and focus on Bessie.

"You've gotten worse," she announced, matter-of-factly. "You cannot go on like this."

Embarrassed, Bessie looked about as though she was concerned, they might be overheard.

"Please, Miss Sarah," she begged. "I would not wish for Mr. Smith to learn of my ailment."

The mere mention of the manager's name caused Sarah's skin to crawl, and she hastily looked about, half-expecting him to be lurking in the shadows.

"Come along now," she mumbled, suddenly in a rush to leave. She did not wish to be cornered by Derrick Smith on this evening.

Bessie took hold of herself, and the pair headed out into the cool night, welcoming the fresh but foul-scented air. The smell of the factory clung to them both, regardless of how often they washed. Baths were fewer and further between than they had ever been for both women, but Sarah reasoned she had little need for washing. There was no one to impress but Derrick Smith who did not much seem to mind if Sarah had not bathed for weeks on end. But for the ribbon she still wore every day as a reminder of William, there was little to remember the Sarah Joyce who had once lived a life of finery.

"Miss Sarah—"

"Bessie, you must stop calling me that," Sarah chided the older woman gently for what seemed to be the thousandth time.

"Forgive me, Miss," Bessie mumbled, another small fit of coughing punctuating her words. "Old habits die hard."

Sarah could not be cross with the woman. She was fond of Bessie in myriad ways. Sometimes she considered her a mother figure whilst other times, the former servant was simply her best friend, despite the age difference. Bessie was very close to fifty now and Sarah a mere seventeen years old.

The pair slowed their gait as they neared the poor house where they shared a room, neither in a rush to be confined within its crumbling walls. Yet exhaustion prevailed and hunger too, the pair sharing barely two shillings between them. The cost of board left little for food and they had already stretched their expenses as far as they could manage. Pay would not be for another two days.

"Go on ahead," Sarah offered when Bessie gave the house a wary glance. "You should get off your feet and rest."

Bessie's eyes widened in dismay.

"You know I do not care for you wandering about in the dark, Miss—Sarah," she corrected herself.

"I won't wander," Sarah promised. "I merely wish to take in the air a moment or two. Please, Bessie. Do go and rest. I'll be along shortly."

The older woman parted her lips to argue but another wracking cough prevented her.

"Eat the last of the potatoes and onions," Sarah added, ignoring her own rumbling belly. She had learned to make do without food for days at a time. Bessie needed it far more than she.

"Do not linger long," Bessie rasped when her fit subsided, but she did not hesitate. Sarah stared after her a long while, her heart heavying in the aftermath.

Above her head, she heard the sobs of a woman, a man's angry voice demeaning her for improperly washed clothes. From another house down the alleyway, a baby shrieked. In the shadows beyond, a lady of the night strolled shamelessly through the streets, pausing to peer at any man who gave her a look. Sarah often wondered about these women. Most would turn up their noses and sneer at their wanton ways, but Sarah secretly envied their bravery.

Certainly, it is easier than enduring the abuses of the mills, she reasoned although she had no true knowledge of what their jobs entailed. She imagined herself away from the likes of Angela and Gertrude, but she was certain entertaining men in scandalous ways surely had its difficulties.

A waft of air filled her nostrils and Sarah was struck with a chord of melancholy. The scent reminding her of Joseph and William, a breeze of the sea commingled with something elusive.

Tears filled her eyes and she struggled to keep them at bay but between her extreme tiredness and general malaise of the soul, they slipped down her cheeks. It was the real reason she had wanted a moment to herself. She did not want for Bessie to witness her sobbing, as she did so many nights, longing for the family she had lost to the cruel sea.

Teddy, Joseph...William...

How much more loss could she be expected to endure?

So often, she laid awake, terrified by Bessie's strained coughs, pondering what she would do if Bessie were to die also.

I could not bear it, she thought, pressing her lips together and willing herself to clear her eyes. Yet Sarah reasoned that she had already survived the loss of those she had loved the most and now, she merely existed without purpose or reason.

"Miss Sarah!"

Bessie's head appeared from above, her long hair spilling from the window ledge.

"I'm coming, Bessie." She sighed, wiping at her face and turning her head lest the woman read her anguish.

Bessie was lying on the bed by the time Sarah reached the second floor, her breathing sounding wheezy.

She sounds like Father, before he passed.

"Come to bed, Miss," Bessie urged without turning. "We've to be at the mill again in the morning."

"Yes, I am aware," Sarah muttered. Bessie flipped over and eyed her; her lips pursed.

"What is it, Bessie?" She knew when the woman was holding her tongue.

"I..." she paused and averted her eyes. "I would not like you to think I am speaking out of turn, Miss Sarah."

"Bessie, you should know better by now."

"It seems to me that Mr. Smith pays you a good deal of attention," she blurted out. The mention of his name sent an unpleasant wave of goosebumps over Sarah.

"Indeed, he does," she agreed, pivoting away from the bed to unravel her long, blonde braid. Tenderly, she untied the ribbon, careful to fold it and cut away any of the fraying ends before laying it against the vanity which held a basin of water. She caught sight of her tired face in the cracked glass of the mirror but did not dwell on the unfamiliar face she saw looking back at her.

"He does well for himself as the manager," Bessie continued, emboldened. "And he is unmarried."

Bessie's implication was clear, and Sarah did not fault her for the suggestion. A woman in her position had few options and Bessie only wished the best for Sarah. Yet a spark of indignation spiked down her spine and she shook her head vehemently.

"If I were to resign myself to marriage, I would prefer a man, not a snivelling boy," she cried with far more harshness than she intended. Bessie balked and Sara was immediately contrite.

"I know you mean well," she added quickly, flashing Bessie a smile she did not feel.

"You could do worse, you know," Bessie squeaked.

"Not by much," Sarah grouched, slipping out of her soiled dress and into her nightclothes. Bessie made no comment but shoved over a little to allow Sarah to lie at her side. In less than a minute, the older woman's breaths deepened, the nasal rasp loudening to keep Sarah on alert.

She cannot be working in the mill much longer, Sarah thought worriedly. *If I were to marry Derrick Smith, it would enable her to leave that life behind and she could work as my maid.*

She swallowed the thickness forming in her own chest, the days' fibres settling against her lungs and filling her mouth with actual cotton. Ensuring that Bessie was soundly asleep, at least for the moment, she rose again and poured herself a glass of water, drowning the specks of dust in her windpipe before blowing out the single candle that flickered against the draughty room. Sarah stood in the dark, unmoving.

What has my life become? A choice between a slow, painful death in the mills or one as equally agonising as the wife of Derrick Smith.

The latter certified a healthier existence for herself and for Bessie, but would it truly be worth the sacrifice? Her mind moved to the day ahead, another shift filled with ridicule and demanding labour. She could see Angela sneering and feel her hands wearing down, threatening arthritis at the age of seventeen.

Her cerulean irises rested on Bessie once more, her heart heavy with longing.

If only William had returned to us, she thought miserably. *I never truly ever told him what he meant to me.*

A steel rod stiffened her spine, and a snide voice reprimanded her.

You are no longer a little girl, Sarah Joyce. You must stop wallowing in the past.

Her choices were grim, but she was still alive—even if the love of her life was dead and gone from her.

Bessie began to cough, and Sarah rushed forward to tend to the woman. There was no choice. She had to get herself and Bessie free of the terrible life they had found before she lost the last person in the world who cared for her.

CHAPTER 8

The day dragged on with its usual tediousness, lack of sleep and general hunger causing Sarah's mind to filter away from her task to better times.

She was distinctly aware of Derrick Smith watching her from his elevated office, attempting to catch her eye every time she lifted her head. Sarah quickly learned to keep her eyes averted.

How odd that he manages to stare so intently but does not appear to see Angela and Gertrude when they shove me roughly.

Of course, Sarah understood that Derrick must see the actions of the other women but chose not to involve himself. He was not renowned for his courage.

Suddenly, a cry forced the girl to whirl about, the sound rising above the din of the machines, prickling her skin as she recognised the pitch and tone of Bessie's yelp. Sarah's eyes tore about the factory for her friend. A small crowd of women had gathered around and without thinking, Sarah abandoned her post, her legs carrying as fast as she could move toward the sight.

"Stop the machine!" someone cried out and Sarah quickly understood why. The hem of Bessie's skirt was tangled in the machinery; her sinewy frame being yanked toward the cogs. The younger woman shoved everyone from her path, reaching Bessie in seconds.

"Bessie!" she breathed, aghast by the sight. "You must pull!"

Terrified, Bessie looked towards her, her face pale and her chin quivering but her shock prevented her from struggling. Sarah seized her arm and yanked as hard as she could, ignoring Bessie's yowl of pain.

"Bessie," she urged vying to keep her voice even. "You'll be pulled through if you do not fight against it. Please, pull!"

Again, she wrenched her friend, noting how little the other women did.

They would see us harmed rather than help, she realised, sickened by the notion. Her shoulder popped with the second effort, but Sarah barely noticed, Bessie's body inching toward the sharp cogs of the machine. The third attempt nearly fully dislocating her shoulder from its socket, but the tearing of Bessie's skirt was a welcome sound and the pair tumbled to the ground. Sarah's head impacted the floor, a wave of dizziness overcoming her as Bessie piled on top of her. The woman began to sob, her body trembling with relief.

"Are you hurt?" Sarah gasped, ignoring her own searing agony as they righted themselves. "Look at me!"

Bessie's dark eyes blurred with tears as Sarah searched her face for signs of injury, but she saw no blood or indications of any broken bones.

"Miss Sarah!" Bessie gasped, her irises bugging when the pair rose. "Your arm."

"It's fine," Sarah lied, backing away.

"What is the meaning of this?" Derrick Smith appeared at the scene, causing Sarah to grit her teeth together.

"I was pushed into the machine," Bessie explained quickly, looking about for the offender of the chaos.

"It was an accident," Gertrude Morrison whined, a malicious twinkle in her eyes. Sarah inhaled, steeling herself from advancing on the woman. "I didn't mean te bump ye."

"Get back to work, the lot of you!" Derrick barked, his eyes lingering on Sarah. The younger woman glanced at Bessie who shook her head.

"Miss Sarah's arm—" she began but Sarah cast her a warning look. She could not afford to be sent away.

"My arm is fine," Sarah said again firmly.

"It don't look fine," Angela chortled. "It's all out of place."

"Mind your own affairs, Angela," Sarah spat, her eyes narrowing dangerously. "I'm just as competent with one arm as I am with two."

She did not hide the naked threat. Angela sneered but did not push the issue and when Derrick attempted to corner Sarah, she hurried back to her station, purposely ignoring him. She was in no mood to deal with him or anyone else when she felt so poorly.

Yet as the day progressed, the pain in her arm and head increased, blinding her vision and making it difficult for her to focus. She made mistakes and was immediately called out by the other women.

"You're doing more harm than good!" one of the workers complained. She was not someone with whom Sarah typically had a problem, but her poor work ethic brought out ridicule in all the others now that she was incapable of performing to her full capacity.

"You're no good to us here," another insisted. "Leave us. You're only making more work!"

There was a murmur of consensus, but Sarah refused to give up her place. She did not need to think about what even one day of lost wages would mean. Her stomach grumbled, reminding her that she had not eaten that day nor the one before.

I must keep working. There is no other option.

Several times during her shift, she found herself dizzy, pausing in her tasks to wipe the sweat from her brow with her good arm. The swelling in her right shoulder restricted her movements and made her wince but she dared not allow anyone to see her discomfort.

"Poor princess," Angela jeered, striding by. "Where's yer servant te help ye with yer work?"

Flustered and frustrated, Sarah blinked away her tears of agony, her jaw twitching as she willed Angela to continue through. The urge to strike the smug woman in the face was overwhelming but she dared not.

"No answer today, princess?" Angela continued, pausing by Sarah's station. "Surely ye 'ave something te say?"

Sarah's eyes darted toward the office and as always, Derrick stood, watching the floor below. She gazed at him imploringly, willing him to come down and put an end to Angela's taunting but the skinny, bucktoothed man remained by the window, his eyes fixed on Sarah.

A fine husband he would make, she thought bitterly. *He hasn't a managerial bone in his body.*

"Did ye hit yer tongue when ye took yer spill?" Angela pressed. Sarah whipped her head around.

"I've struck you once already, Angie. Do not have me do it again. It will not bode as well for you this time."

Angela appeared to sense her weakness, her smirk widening.

"I'd like te see ye try," she barked, folding her arms over her smock, her gaze challenging. More tears and vertigo overcame Sarah.

Please God, don't permit me to fall down here, in front of everyone.

The long whistle ricocheted through the warehouse, indicating the end of their shift. Sarah could hardly believe that she had endure it in her position.

"Come along, Miss," Bessie breathed, arriving at her side even before Sarah could turn away to search for her. She linked her arm through Sarah's left and helped the younger woman toward the exit.

"Miss Joyce!"

Sarah cringed at the sound of her name, knowing who it was that called out to her.

"You might pretend you didn't hear him," Bessie suggested but Sarah stopped in her tracks as Derrick Smith hurried toward her.

Now he comes down from his ivory tower, she mused with exasperation. Sarah did not miss the look of contempt Angela flashed them before gathering her skirts and heading away.

"Could I have a word?" Derrick asked, taking Sarah's arm before she could respond. Bessie stared helplessly at the pair as the manager all but dragged her off, but Sarah did not put up a fight. She was far too exhausted, weak, and pained to struggle.

Into the night, Derrick guided them, finding a private corner against the building. To her left, Sarah saw the streams of workers leaving their shifts, no one paying a bit of mind to the shadowy figures in the darkness.

"You were hurt," Derrick announced. The girl pursed her lips, swallowing a snarky reply. She did not mention that her injury had occurred hours earlier and that she had since been subjected to cruelty under his watch.

"I managed," she replied instead, averting her eyes away. "You needn't worry about my ability to work."

"Oh, but I do!" he declared, stepping closer. His breath smelled of fish and staleness, the aftermath of tobacco wafting from his lips. Until that moment, Sarah had not realised he was a smoker, but it explained the yellow stain of his teeth. She drew back subtly, lowering her eyes as she did.

"I very much need this employment, Mr. Smith," she told him honestly. "I endured my shift without complaint."

"Ah, but you should not need to work at all, Miss Joyce." He leered, his upper lip curling over his uneven teeth, his head dipping closer. "A comely girl like you with her fine upbringing should not be made to work the mills."

Sarah inhaled and choked down the rush of bile in her throat.

"I fear that is the only option for now," she demurred, understanding the point of his private meeting. Through her peripheral vision, she saw Bessie waiting, her head straining forward as if she were attempting to see their features and hear their words.

She cannot see much from where she stands but she dares not come closer.

Still, it was great comfort to know that her friend was near even if there was little that Bessie could do from her position.

"That is not so, and you know it," Derrick rasped, leaning in closer, his breath hot and uncomfortable against Sarah's skin. The now-familiar goosebumps spiked her flesh, but she did not move, a lump forming in her throat. She thought of Bessie's words earlier in the week, the prospect of entertaining a life with Derrick Smith. Demurely, Sarah looked away, waiting for him to fully announce his intentions.

"I should not have to tell you about my feelings towards you, Sarah. I believe I've made them very clear over the past years."

Still, Sarah said nothing, upset churning her stomach, the smell of the man repulsing her. The mere pitch of his nasal tone would have been enough to send her running in another direction at another time in her life, but Sarah was well aware that she was no longer the same young lady.

"Marry me, Sarah." Spittle sprayed from Derrick's mouth as he spoke the words. "You'll never have to work again. You'll bear my sons and keep my house, just as God intended for a girl as lovely as you."

She could not stifle the shudder but managed to hide it. Derrick was far too invested in his nearness to notice, a calloused hand stroking at the skin of her cheek. Sarah wanted nothing more than to scream and curse, order him away from her but her gaze again fell on Bessie who hovered near the road. The older woman's coughing echoed through the alleyway, reminding Sarah that her choices affected Bessie also.

"Could I take a servant? My friend, Bessie Mulligan?"

"Yes, of course," Derrick grumbled impatiently, lips brushing against her face. "Or perhaps someone younger."

"No!" Sarah backed up and Derrick's face registered disappointment. A scowl overtook his features.

"Fine, Mrs. Mulligan will suffice," he growled, pulling her back toward him, not mindful of her injury. She winced but Derrick did not notice, his mouth finding hers now. Repelled, Sarah closed her eyes and permitted the kiss to occur.

"You deserve better than this, Sarah," Derrick murmured, a hand sliding along the back of her dress. Sarah wiggled out of his grasp and exhaled a breath she had not realised she was holding. His frown deepened.

"Where are you going?"

"I-I need a night to consider your generous offer," she mumbled, her mind racing. She did not wish to offend him.

"Consider what?" he snapped. "Who else would offer you better?"

"No one," Sarah agreed quickly, tilting her head toward him demurely. "But I am very tired and partially hurt, Mr. Smith. Please, do permit me to take your offer with a clear head and not made out of desperation."

She held his stare evenly, half-challenging him to argue with her reasoning. He balked slightly, his eyes narrowing but he did not reach for her again.

"Very well. I've waited two years. I imagine I can wait another day. I will expect your answer in the morning."

Sarah nodded, gulping back the thickness in her throat.

"You shall have it," she agreed, slipping fully out of his hold to back down through the alleyway. "Goodnight, Mr. Smith."

"Miss Joyce."

She spun and rushed toward Bessie who appeared deeply relieved.

"What was that about?" the former servant demanded as they rushed out of earshot. The remnants of Derrick's kiss burned into Sarah's lips, and she wiped at her mouth vigorously.

A lifetime with Derrick Smith, she thought miserably. *Is this what my life has become?*

"Miss Sarah?"

"He's formally requested my hand in marriage," she explained hastily. Bessie inhaled sharply but Sarah did not look at her.

"What did you say, Miss?"

"That I need a night to consider his offer," Sarah muttered. She did not add that she suspected she already knew what her answer would be. "Come along, Bessie. I must find something to eat tonight."

"Not to speak of your arm, Miss Sarah. It's getting worse, I daresay."

Sarah could barely move her shoulder now but the pain in her heart was far worse than that in her extremities.

I am still a little girl of five, trapped, alone and afraid, she told herself, blinking away the tears in her eyes. There would be no Joseph Tavers to save her life this time. Now, Sarah had to save herself and Bessie the only way she could.

CHAPTER 9

A fit of coughing roused Bessie from her slumber, the sound commonplace to her ears. It was her own, of course, and desperate as she was to stop it, specks of spittle flew from her mouth as she turned away from Miss Sarah to keep from spraying her. After the moment had passed, she came to realise that the younger woman was not asleep at her side as she expected but curled in the rickety chair near the window, peering outside.

"Miss?" Bessie whispered, sitting up fully to take in the moonlight cascading over the young woman's pale face. "Are you well?"

Miss Sarah did not turn towards her, sending spikes of worry through Bessie's already frail heart. Tears glistened on her cheeks as Bessie neared, the girl sniffling desperately to hide her condition from the servant.

"Oh, Miss. Are you in pain?"

Sarah shook her loose, blonde curls that were sticking to her damp face. She ran her left hand over her cheeks but did little to conceal her inner turmoil with the gesture.

Bessie hurried to fetch a glass of water but when she offered it to Sarah refused.

"You take it, Bessie," she murmured, her voice raspy and indicative of hours of misery. "There's little left and your cough is worsening."

Stubbornly, Bessie insisted until Sarah's hand curled around the glass, and she took a half-hearted sip to placate Bessie before setting the cup onto the floor at her feet. Bessie noted how limply her left side sat and in the poor lighting of the moon, she saw the swelling.

"Miss Sarah, your shoulder…" she whispered, unsure of what to do. There simply was no money to call for a doctor and if there had been, she was certain Sarah would have used it on her cough long ago.

"Please, don't cry, Miss," Bessie begged, knowing that her words had little comfort. "You are young and healthy. I'm certain the pain will subside in good time."

"No," Sarah sniffed. "It is not the pain that plagues me, Bessie."

Understanding flooded the older woman and she sat on the floor, near Sarah's legs. Immediately, she rose to offer the chair, but Bessie declined the offer.

"I'm quite comfortable here," she fibbed, urging the girl back onto the splintered, wooden seat. "Do sit and tell me what troubles you."

Reluctantly, Sarah reclaimed her spot, pursing her rosebud lips together before again turning her attention out the window.

"I've promised to give Mr. Smith a response to his proposal tomorrow," she reminded Bessie. "It's a daunting decision."

Guilt smothered Bessie's heart as she recalled her own advice to the young woman. Having never married herself, it had been unfair of her to suggest that Sarah wed the manager, particularly when it appeared to cause her so much distress. Another tear slid down Sarah's cheek and Bessie impulsively raised a hand to wipe it away as she had so many times in the girl's youth.

Their eyes met and Bessie read the clear anguish of her position.

"I spoke out of turn the other night," the servant breathed, brushing her cheek affectionately. "No one should be made to wed anyone they do not choose."

"It is not so simple, and you know that, Bessie."

Bessie closed her mouth, a deep discomfort aching through her bones. Her condition weakened her further every day and though she did her best to hide her ailments from Sarah, she knew she could not endure the work at the cotton mill for much longer. Her life had been committed to servitude under the gentle care of Joseph Tavers. As she approached the age of fifty, her body was ill-equipped to handle the ways of factory work, desperate as she was to make money. Even with her pay at the factory, she and Miss Sarah were destitute. There was barely enough to sustain the pair with the two incomes.

"If I were to marry Mr. Smith, you would come to keep house with me," Sarah explained. Bessie loathed the ignition of hope that the words sparked in her heart. It was clear that her mistress did not wish to marry Mr. Smith.

"You must do what is proper for yourself, Miss, not me," Bessie said, lowering her head. "I will make do regardless of my circumstance."

"We will make do together," Miss Sarah replied firmly but her words cracked, and she blinked rapidly.

"What can I do to ease your suffering, Miss?"

Sarah smiled thinly, not a modicum of mirth attached to her expression.

"Could you see Will brought back to us?" she whispered. "Could you pray with me and have God return him from the depths of the ocean?"

Bessie's eyes burned, not with exhaustion but sadness, as she recognised precisely what weighed so heavily on Sarah.

"He never knew," she went on, losing herself in the memory of years gone. "How I felt about him, truly. He went away and I never had the opportunity to tell him that I cared for him, differently than that of a brother."

"Oh, Miss," Bessie cried softly, reaching for the young woman's hand. "I'm certain he knew. It was clear in the way you followed him around, in the looks you gave him. He must have sensed your feelings for him."

She buried her face in her hands and permitted herself to sob freely now.

"Why is God so cruel?" she whimpered between her heaving breaths. "Why does He take those whom I love away?"

Bessie had no answer for the heartbroken girl, Sarah's confessions startling but understandable. The year which had taken Joseph from the children had created a bond between them. Bessie had noticed the closeness but she had truly never suspected how much Sarah had come to love William.

She has lost so much at such a young age. She must not subject herself to more loss.

Bessie said as much aloud, and the words caused Sarah to raise her head abruptly. Streaks zigzagged down her face as she stared intently at the servant with crimson-rimmed eyes.

"You're right, Bessie," she rasped. "I cannot afford to lose anyone else."

Uncertainly, Bessie returned her look.

"Marrying Mr. Smith is the only way to ensure our futures," she continued. It was not the response that Bessie had expected, and it filled her with some dread.

"But Miss, you do not much care for him."

"My mother did not much care for my father and yet she married him," the girl replied, her eyes widening as if recollecting the horrors of her early childhood. "Many wed simply because it is the right thing to do."

"I'm unsure if I agree," Bessie mumbled worriedly. "You are very young yet, Miss, a comely, bright lady. There will undoubtedly be other suitors…"

She trailed off, her confidence wavering. Perhaps when they lived in the Tavers' home, Miss Sarah's prospects would have been better, but now? Who else could Miss Sarah possibly entertain as a proper husband?

"I highly doubt that." Sarah sighed, reading Bessie's thoughts clearly. "Moreover, should I keep him waiting, he will certainly find another to court. I must decide tonight, Bessie."

"Then you should decide no." This time when Bessie spoke, there was surety to her statement. Miss Sarah was silent for a long moment, her eyes trailing back toward the window. A grey light began to filter through the darkness, indicating that morning was nigh.

"Come back to sleep," Bessie urged, rising wearily from her spot on the floor. Her bones creaked with the effort and another spasm of coughing wracked through her.

"You go ahead," Sarah mumbled, making no move to stand from her own place. "I could not rest."

"Miss Sarah, you cannot undo the past. I would like nothing more than for Mr. Tavers and Master William to be here with us, but God has called them both to His side. I know that neither would wish to see you unhappy."

"Nor you, Bessie."

"Nor I," she agreed. "We must not dwell on what is unattainable. They are gone but God has spared us. As you say, we will make do—together."

Miss Sarah cast her a sidelong look but did not speak and Bessie was granted no other option but to return to the bed.

"I'll rest a little longer," she said, stifling a yawn.

"I'll wake you when it's time," Sarah told her as she crawled back onto the lumpy, straw mattress and pulled the holey quilt toward her chin. She was asleep in seconds, despite her sadness.

After what seemed only a few minutes, Bessie was roused by a gentle shaking on her arm.

"It's time to wake now, Bessie."

Blinking, she stared up at Sarah's pale, drawn face. Sunlight poured weakly through the windows and Sarah wore her working dress, her face scrubbed clean of lingering tears. There was a dullness to her cheeks that had not been there before, a look of resignation that troubled Bessie as she sat up.

"Have you rested at all?" she asked chidingly.

"I am fine."

Bessie slipped off the mattress and hurried to dress, unsure of the time but motivated by Sarah's presentation.

"Eat something and take the last of the water," Sarah instructed. When Bessie began to argue, Sarah held up her hand.

"I'll not hear protests," she said firmly. "If all goes well today, we will not be here much longer."

A fusion of worry and relief twisted in Bessie's gut as she gazed at her mistress.

"Miss?"

Visibly swallowing, Sarah averted her eyes.

"I've made my decision," she announced. "I will accept Mr. Smith's proposal this morning."

CHAPTER 10

It had been Sarah's intention to work her shift and speak privately to Derrick following her workday. She did not know how long an engagement the man would insist upon nor how soon she might take Bessie along with her. She also longed to have the extra time to build her courage in accepting his ask, the noise and terrible air assisting in her motivation.

Unfortunately, Derrick Smith waited at her station, the moment she arrived, causing the other women to cast her sly, contemptuous glances.

"Miss Joyce, I'd like a private word," he announced loudly enough for all to hear. Gulping back her nervousness, Sarah nodded and permitted him to lead her upstairs into the office from which he had watched her for two long years.

It was the first time that Sarah had ever been inside the small, cramped room but with the door secured, the din of the factory was considerably less and the quality of air much more endurable.

I see why he prefers to stand here all day, she mused, taking in the view of her workers. Their stares were hard and annoyed, fuelling her decision. It would be a relief not to see Angela Yates and Gertrude Morrison every day. There was an end in sight, even if it were distant.

"Have you given any thought to our discussion last eve?" Derrick asked, nearing her. Sarah stepped away from the windows and offered him a taut smile.

"I have."

"You did promise me a response today."

"I did," she agreed. "And…"

She hesitated, eyeing his porcine face.

Good Lord. What if our children take after him?

"Well?" He did not hide the impatience in his voice.

"I accept your proposal." She was unable to add a jot of enthusiasm to her words, but Derrick did not appear to notice her lacklustre agreement. A wide smile broke over his features, pig-like nostrils flaring outward as he moved in to kiss her on the mouth again. She abruptly turned her head and his lips landed on her cheek.

"I knew you would!" He laughed, pulling back to grin, flashing his yellowing teeth. His nearness encompassed her in another cloud of tobacco, the smell gagging her slightly. "I'll inform the foreman of your termination immediately."

Sarah balked.

"Oh, no I…I must continue to work," she sputtered. "Until we're married. How else will I afford room and board?"

"You'll move into my house at once," he scoffed as though she asked a ridiculous question. "I'll not have my betrothed living in a rooming house."

Sarah paled more.

"But—but—" she stammered. "The impropriety!"

Derrick snorted and arched a blonde eyebrow.

"I would not have thought you would pay much attention to what others thought, Sarah," he chided. "Despite your upbringing, you do not live in high society any longer, do you? If anyone should care about propriety, it is me and I insist you move into my house at once—assuming of course, you wish to marry."

Sarah's heart hammered as she considered his words.

"You needn't concern yourself with sleeping arrangements," he added, sensing her hesitation. "You'll have a room of your own—until we can be married."

Relief swept through her, and she nodded slowly.

"And Bessie Mulligan?"

"Who?"

Sarah swallowed her exasperation.

"You did say I could bring Bessie Mulligan with me when we married."

Derrick grimaced slightly but caught the steel in Sarah's eyes. Grunting he shrugged.

"She may come along after we've married. I haven't the space for her and yourself in separate rooms. If you would like to share my bed, that is another tale entirely."

Sarah gasped aloud and backed away, shaking her head in disgust.

"Certainly not!" she declared, not caring if her tone was stern. "I will do no such thing!"

Derrick's face twisted, concern colouring his sallow complexion. He smiled briefly and forced a laugh.

"That was a joke, Sarah, of course."

She remained near the door, studying his face with new eyes.

"I will not move out of my rooming house without Bessie. She cannot afford it alone and I will not abandon her."

Derrick met her eyes evenly, but Sarah sensed that he would not cave on this matter.

"I promised that Mrs. Mulligan could come to stay after we are wed," he insisted. "Until there is room for her—"

"I could share a room with her," Sarah pleaded. "It is how we manage now. It will be no inconvenience."

"The best I can offer is a slight increase in her wages here," Derrick suggested slowly. "It will enable her to keep her room until she is employed at my house."

Sarah glanced back down toward the floor below. Bessie's head tilted upward, the concern in her eyes palpable, even from the distance between them.

"How much of an increase?"

"Enough to keep her until we are married." His annoyance rang in Sarah's ears. "Truly, you are making this more difficult than it need be."

"All right," she breathed before she could change her mind. "I'll collect my belongings after my shift and inform Bessie."

"There is no need to complete your shift and I will speak with Mrs. Mulligan directly. I'll have a carriage bring you directly home and a driver collect your things. Come along, I'll see you out."

Sarah's lips parted to argue but Derrick had already marched forward, throwing open the door and allowing the deafening noise of the factory inside.

"Please, let me say goodbye to Bessie!" Sarah begged but Derrick did not appear to hear her as he guided her away from the servant toward the back exit. Desperately, Sarah looked for her friend, but all saw was Angela Yate's scowling face, the expression causing the girl to wither inside.

They will all hear about this and be crueller to Bessie for it, she realised, hoping to explain her concerns to Derrick. Yet when she attempted to tell him, he merely ushered her into a waiting carriage.

"I haven't time for chitchat, Sarah," he barked crossly. "I've a job to do."

He turned his attention to the driver and ordered him to take her home, mentioning nothing of her belongings.

"You'll speak with Bessie?" Sarah called out as the horse pulled away from the alley, trailing the carriage in his wake. Derrick did not acknowledge her question, hurrying back into the building as she drove off.

Sarah sat back, biting on her lower lip.

To what have I agreed? she wondered worriedly. It was too late to do anything about it now. She would wait for Derrick to return to the house that night and speak with him more when he did.

~

Derrick Smith owned a small, stone cottage on the edge of Bromley, a twenty-minute carriage ride from Wallopher's Textile Factory.

The gardens were ill-kept, overgrown with climbing weeds and overrun with ivy that reached out to grab at Sarah like tentacles as she entered the front door. The driver had not bothered to see her inside, dropping her off at the road without so much as a tip of his hat.

"Hello?" Sarah called timidly as she pushed open the door. A swirl of dust assaulted her nostrils, but it was nothing in comparison to the floating wafts of cotton fibres she inhaled every day.

"Hello? Is anyone here?"

Only silence met her ears, the lack of sound both reassuring and unnerving. There were no maids or butlers in this house that was coated in dust and cobwebs. A trail of crumbs and mouse droppings proved that nothing more than vermin resided there with Derrick.

A closer inspection found two bedrooms and a smaller, suffocating maid's chamber which Sarah could not bear to imagine for Bessie. Filthy dishes piled high in the kitchen basin, a scatter of feet reaching her ears as she neared the cupboards. It was a dirty house, but it was a house, one which did not bear the threat of eviction once she and Derrick were married. It was far smaller than the Tavers' estate, but Sarah was certain she could make this building into a home.

She discovered a third and fourth room at the back of the house, each one filled to the brim with rubbish of sorts. Wood pieces and knickknacks, crates and trunks, all piled atop one another as if Derrick had inherited another house.

Still, there was more space than Sarah first envisioned and her heart leapt to think that Bessie could move in sooner than expected if she merely cleared out some of the rubbish.

Sarah got to work, cleaning and organising as she waited for Derrick to finish his shift and return home. She hoped to impress him with her domestic skills and soften his attitude toward bringing Bessie along before they were officially married. She did not like the notion of living alone with Derrick. The neighbours were sure to talk, and it made Sarah feel unclean.

Yet Derrick is correct. I'm no lady to speak of. I've no right to worry about propriety.

She was exhausted by day's end and collapsed upon the couch in the front room. Her stomach complained, hunger overtaking her, but she quickly learned that there was nothing but rotten fruit in the kitchen.

I'll have Derrick leave me some money for groceries and make him a lovely supper tomorrow, she vowed, determined to be a good partner to the man, despite her misgivings about the situation. He had still provided her with a future, something she had not been certain of mere days before. She could not fault him for not being William, the only man who would ever truly have her heart. Bessie had been right about the Tavers men wanting the best for them and, in this situation, the best was Derrick Smith.

Night fell over the house and Sarah lit a lamp, careful to be sparing with the kerosene. She did not need much light to read by the window, locating a small stack of books in one of the rooms.

But after a short time, she could no longer keep her eyes from falling closed, realising as she drifted off that no one had brought her clothes and other belongings from the rooming house.

A loud crash woke her abruptly and Sarah gasped, forgetting where she was as her eyes fluttered open. Derrick stumbled through the door, falling into the couch where she sat, forcing Sarah upward in a scurry.

"Mr. Smith!" she choked, alarmed to see him in such a state. "Are you ill?"

He leered at her and instantly, she recognised his intoxication, the smell of cigarettes and whiskey oozing from his pores.

"I've been celebrating my betrothment," he jeered, flopping onto his back. "Come and give us a kiss, luv."

Gone was his proper way of speaking, his words slurring and nonsensical as they fell on one another. Sarah wrinkled her nose and shook her head.

"I've been waiting for you to return," she told him accusingly. "No one has returned with my things from the boarding house."

Derrick waved a hand and moved to rise but his inebriation stalled his movements and he fell back against the cushioning.

"Do you like my house?"

"I...yes. It's quite charming," Sarah answered slowly. Memories of her own father rushed through her mind, seeing Derrick in such a state. "I've done what I could—"

She abruptly stopped speaking as she noticed his eyes had fallen closed, his head tipped to the side.

"Mr. Smith?"

A loud snore vibrated from his chest and Sarah stared at him in the darkness, unsure of what to do. She did not wish to leave him sprawled half on the couch but the idea of removing his clothes made her shudder. She settled with laying him horizontally against the couch and taking off his boots, wriggling her nose in disgust at the scent of him. Satisfied that he would not fall, she backed away, one eye still on him as though she expected him to rise and lunge for her where she stood. In the shadowy black, he looked nothing like she recalled of her father, the violent brute who was at least twice as big as Derrick Smith, yet the scent of booze triggered a deeply rooted memory that curled her gut and forced her back into the rear of the house.

She found herself in the tiny servant bedroom, huddling against the door as she reclaimed her breaths.

He is not my father, and I am being ridiculous, she chided herself, rocking against the hard cot. Yet she closed herself inside the room, daring to breathe as quietly as possible in the windowless chamber until she could wait no longer and fell back into a fitful, terrified sleep.

∼

"Have you taken leave of your senses?"

Sarah's eyes popped open at the harsh question, Derrick's irritated face looming over her on the bed. Inhaling, she reached to cover herself but remembered she still wore her working dress. Gone was the drunken fool she had helped to bed the previous night and in his place was the arrogant manager she had always known.

"No…" she replied quietly.

"Why would you sleep in a cupboard when I have a room for you?" he scowled. On closer inspection, it was clear that Derrick was worse for wear, his eyes bleary and his face unshaven. Although he had managed to comb his wiry blonde hair, he smelt of the gutters.

"I-I wasn't certain which room was mine," Sarah fibbed, straightening herself. "My belongings never arrived yesterday."

Derrick huffed and spun away.

"I must leave for the factory. I would have hoped for breakfast—or tea at minimum."

"There's little in the way of food here," Sarah called out to his retreating back, rising to keep pace with him. "I had hoped to do a bit of shopping while you were at work."

He paused and glanced back at her, eyes narrowing.

"You'll stay put," he growled. "Do you want the neighbours to blather about you?"

Stunned, Sarah gaped at him. It had been her very same concern only the previous day and he had dismissed it!

"I-I would like to make you a nice supper for when you return," she replied, containing her own annoyance. "I cannot without any food in the house."

"Never mind shopping. I'll not give you money to waste frivolously. I do my own shopping on Saturdays, after I'm paid for the week."

Sarah's eyes widened.

"That's three days from now!" she cried. "There's nothing in the house."

"You'll make do," he replied, reaching for the doorknob. "Stay put and do not call attention to yourself."

"Wait!"

He paused and glowered at her.

"What is it? I'll be late!"

"Have you spoken with Bessie? Does she know where I am?"

"I've informed her of your whereabouts, of course," he growled. "What do you take me for?"

Sarah had no answer. She did not know what to make of him. This was half of her problem.

"Now, may I go?" he demanded caustically. "Or have you other trivial matters with which to bombard me?"

"No…" Sarah muttered. "Have a lovely day."

"Unlikely," Derrick growled, slamming the door in his wake. The house reverberated in his aftermath, but it took Sarah several seconds to recognise that it was she who trembled. Pressing her hands together, she inhaled and collected her nerves.

Matters will improve. He is merely blue devilled because of the drink he imbibed. I must not cast waves. I will do as he asks and behave well. Tonight, we will discuss plans for the wedding and bringing Bessie here.

She wished she had her belongings, if only to touch the handkerchief she had taken from Joseph's bedside on the day he had passed. She needed something familiar and kind, anything to still the melancholic ache in her heart.

If she had not been certain that Bessie was at the cotton mill, she would have defied Derrick's orders to see her. She thought about returning to the boarding house if only to retrieve her possessions, but she was worried that it would upset Bessie when the woman returned home from working. If Derrick had not spoken to her, she would surely be perplexed to discover Sarah's belongings gone from their room.

I must sneak off to see her on Sunday, before church, she decided, thinking of no other time when she might get a chance to see Bessie on her own. In the interim, she was left to her own devices, wandering through the small house, cleaning again and devising methods to scare off the mice.

When evening fell again, a newfound apprehension snuck into Sarah's veins.

Will Derrick return amiable or drunk this eve?

She could not decide which was more appealing. Surely if he came home well into his pints, he would fall asleep, thereby sparing her long conversation with his smug countenance. Yet if she were to bind herself to this man forever, was it not better that she get to know him?

Her question was soon answered as the sound of horse's hooves drew her toward the window. A delivery carriage stopped at the road and Derrick jumped from it. The hour was late but not nearly as late as it had been the previous night. Sarah watched his swagger from the window, noting that his steps were even but his air was drunken.

"Where is my wife-to-be?" Derrick cackled, throwing open the door. "Have you taken to the pantry again to sleep?"

"No, Mr. Smith. I'm here," Sarah murmured, rising to greet him, her heart in her throat. He grinned, a familiar leer raking over her face and body, his tongue jutting out to lick at dry lips.

"Won't you give us a kiss and a cuddle?" he asked, and Sarah did not need to smell the liquor to know he was into his cups. His actions were far too bold but more coherent than the previous night.

"Come here," he ordered, striding toward her. "Give us a kiss."

His wet mouth planted on hers, saliva covering her chin. Smothering a yelp, Sarah pulled back, wiping at her face.

"I would rather we keep a respectful distance," she rasped, uneasiness clinging to her gut. "For propriety's sake."

Derrick laughed loudly.

"You've already shacked up in here with me," he reminded her. "What's the difference if we consummate our union now or later?"

Stunned, Sarah gaped at him.

"I would never!" she fired back, insulted by his suggestion.

"You're not the Ton, Miss Joyce," he jeered. "No matter who your papa was. You don't mean to tell me you've never…not once?"

His beady eyes trailed toward her skirts and Sarah gasped, appalled.

"No!" she cried, humiliation washing through her.

"It would not be the first time a comely girl like you has resorted to such tactics for a bit of money," he insisted, drawing her closer. "You can tell me."

Sarah pushed him back, shaking her head vehemently.

"Why would you ever want to marry someone with such poor moral character?" she demanded, blinking away her tears. Derrick sniggered again.

"I would not," he conceded, his smile broadening. "I simply wanted to ensure my investment. It will be that much sweeter now, knowing you are unspoiled."

His hand closed around her wrist, and he yanked her closer.

"We'll be married soon," he purred, his breath hot on her cheek. "There's no reason we should wait another minute."

His mouth brushed over her skin and Sarah shuddered as she realised the extent of her mistake.

I should have never agreed to come here! I should have stayed with Bessie at the boarding house!

Derrick's arm snaked tightly around her waist and another horrifying thought occurred to her.

He had intended to do this last night but got far too drunk!

"No!" she yelled, attempting to push him back but this time, Derrick anticipated her fight and closed his arm tightly around her hip, fingers digging into the tender skin, bruising her.

"You've nowhere else to go, girl," he rasped. "I suggest you don't put up a struggle and make it worse for yourself."

Sarah closed her eyes, praying silently to a God who never, ever listened.

CHAPTER 11

For a man who had lost five years at sea, the week following his arrival on British shores proved the longest of William's life.

He found himself a room at the King George Inn for a nominal sum as he attempted to uncover the truth about his lost family. After a hot bath and meal, he took to the streets for any indication of where Sarah may have gone. He spent the days on the streets of the neighbourhood in which he had been reared, speaking to acquaintances who had known him and his father, but no one had been much use.

"Twas a sad day when I learnt of your father's ailment," Mrs. Buckroy said, nodding as she pruned her roses, a wide-brimmed hat shielding her face from the sun. "He was a dear, dear man."

William bit his tongue to keep himself from reminding the ageing woman how she had been the first to condemn Sarah when Joseph had brought her home.

"I did offer to take the maid into my employ," she added, causing William to perk up with interest. "I know she was quite loyal to Mr. Tavers. Good help is difficult to come by and my own servants were stealing from me."

She sneered slightly at the memory, leaving William to consider she cared more for her lost silverware than those in her employ.

"What did Bessie say to your offer?" William asked, leaning in closer. Mrs. Buckroy sat back and eyed him from her haunches.

"Who?"

"Bessie Mulligan," William snapped, unable to keep his wits about him. "The servant!"

"Oh. Was that what she was called?" Mrs. Buckroy released a tinkling laugh. "They come and go. How can I be expected to keep track?"

"What did Bessie tell you, Mrs. Buckroy?" There was ice in William's tone, enough to turn the woman's nose upward indignantly.

"She had the gall to demand I offer the urchin a job also," she sniffed. "Naturally, I declined."

William's temper flared.

"Do you mean Sarah?" he growled, certain that was precisely who she meant. "Is she the urchin you speak of?"

"Oh, come now, Mr. Tavers. You must know that despite the education your father bestowed upon the girl, she was a ship rat from the colonies. I fear your father's heart was larger than his good sense."

William's hands closed into fists at his sides and while he would never consider striking a woman, Mrs. Buckroy was wearing on his last nerve.

"Where did they go?" he asked through clenched teeth. "Surely someone must know."

The elegant older woman sighed heavily as though the conversation was draining her.

"I could not say, Mr. Tavers. I heard that the servant had family somewhere about. An uncle perhaps?"

William inhaled sharply.

Of course! Alfred Mulligan!

It had been a decade or more since William had last seen Bessie's kin, but he remembered the kindly man well. Could Bessie have gone to stay with him and brought Sarah with her? It was the first inkling of hope that William had felt in days. The man must be an age by now but it was worth looking for him, in case he knew where Bessie had gone. William deeply suspected that Bessie had remained with Sarah, her loyalty undeniable.

"Good day, Mrs. Buckroy," he muttered, spinning away.

"Mr. Tavers," she called out after him. "I would leave well enough alone if I were you. God works in mysterious ways and if He saw fit to send that girl back to the gutter, so be it."

William was unable to contain himself now as he pivoted back and advanced on the woman, sooty eyes flashing indignantly.

"I have traveled the ocean, Mrs. Buckroy and you know what I discovered?"

She smiled unsuspectingly.

"What have you learned, Mr. Tavers?"

"That good fortune often falls to the most undeserving. I daresay that God Himself is ashamed of what He's created here."

Spinning around again he set off at a fast pace.

Now to find Alfred Mulligan. Or have I merely found myself on another wild goose chase?

∼

He found the humble shack by memory, a fact that William was rather proud of. It had taken him hours of winding through the streets, recalling the short trips with Bessie to the East End in his boyhood.

It looked the same as William recalled in his mind's eye, the splintering porch and broken rocker next to an empty barrel of whiskey. The young man's weight caused the wood to creak beneath his boots and William winced, wishing he had come sooner to fix the shanty for Bessie's uncle.

He rapped on the door and listened, pulse quickening as he waited for a response. Heavy, even footfalls sounded hollowly until William stood facing a grey-capped man with yellowing skin.

"Mr. Mulligan," he breathed, relieved to see the man. "Do you remember me?"

Alfred cocked his head, half-blind eyes narrowing as he studied the tall, lean stranger before him.

"William Tavers!" he announced with a laugh. "As I live and breathe, it's truly ye!"

"Indeed, sir." William laughed, relieved that the man still had his faculties in place. He could not help himself from peering over the old man's shoulder for signs of others in the house.

"I'm relieved you remember me, Mr. Mulligan. Please forgive my intrusion, but I've just returned from overseas—"

"They thought ye dead," the man interjected bluntly. "Gone fer years with nary a word. Mourned ye and all, my Bessie did."

William was certain his heart could take no more blows, the stabbing pain doubling him over.

Of course, they thought me dead. The Esmerelda was lost. Oh, my poor, dear Sarah.

"I very nearly perished on several occasions," William confessed. "But God had other plans for me, it seems."

"I reckon ye 'eard of yer father's passin'," Alfred declared solemnly. "I daresay that Bessie had more love for him than she dared admit aloud."

"Mr. Mulligan, what has become of Bessie? Has she been here?"

"Oh, yes." The man chuckled. "She visits weekly to throw me a coin or two when she can but she 'asn't much. She's workin' at the Wallopher Textile plant, last I 'eard, stayin' in one of them poor houses along Abbey Creek. I've never been meself."

He gestured at his wobbling legs, leaning forward on his cane. "I don't get out much these days."

"And Sarah?" he pressed. Alfred cast him a look of confusion, bushy brows knitting to a vee.

"Who would that be?" he asked, frowning.

"It's quite all right, Mr. Mulligan. I'll speak with Bessie directly," he reassured the old timer. "You've been most gracious."

He dug a shilling from his pocket and offered it to the man, but Alfred shook his head.

"Yer family has done more than enough for meself and me kin over the years, Mr. Tavers. I won't take another penny from ye."

Had William the luxury of time, he would have argued with the man, but his palms sweated in anticipation, and he silently vowed to return and assist Alfred at a later date.

"Go now," Alfred said, reading his naked thought. "My Bessie'll be over the moon te see ye. Ye be wary of how ye approach 'er, ye 'ear? Ye'll be liable te give her an apoplexy."

"I will," William promised with a small laugh. "Thank you, Mr. Mulligan."

The door closed and William retraced his steps down the broken stairs toward the winding streets. He knew of the Wallopher Textile factory and found it easily by the time night fell.

Worriedly, he asked a passerby about the changing of shifts but as he posed the question, a loud horn tooted, answering his own question and the stranger wandered off.

A flock of women emerged through the doors in long streams of exhausted, sweaty bodies. William's eyes tore through the crowd, searching for Bessie or Sarah, hope settled upon his sleeve.

"Master William?!"

He whipped around, Bessie's familiar voice warming his heart in ways he could not describe. Tears flooded his eyes to see the woman in such poor state, her once robust cheeks saggy, dark circles ringing about her eyes.

"Is that truly you, Master William?" she gasped, stumbling forward, her pupils dilating.

"Bessie," he choked, extending his hands toward her.

"Y-you were thought dead," Bessie cried, disbelief colouring her face. "H-how can you be here?"

William sighed. "It is a long, terrible tale. But one that can wait until I've located Sarah. Where is she, Bessie? Do you know?"

Deep concern clouded the servant's expression, and a hand flew to her mouth.

"What is it?" William demanded.

"Oh, Master William, you must understand, we believed we had lost everything," she moaned. "Miss Sarah—"

"Whatever it is, I will understand," William promised, dread seizing his gut. "Please, Bessie, where is she?"

Bessie inhaled a shuddering breath, her eyes skipping away from his face.

"She's agreed to marry the day manager and he's keeping her in his house. I haven't seen her in days and frankly, sir, I'm concerned. Her belongings remain at our shared accommodations and—"

William had heard enough.

"Is he here now? This manager?"

Bessie shook her head, her eyes aglow with fright.

"Mr. Smith has left for the day."

"Where does he live?" William's voice rose in a frenzy, his well-honed instincts forewarning him that something was terribly amiss.

Or is this pure jealousy I'm experiencing?

There was no time to ponder the difference.

"I could not say, Master William," Bessie moaned miserably. "I haven't had the occasion to visit."

"Come along," William urged, marching toward the building.

"Master William, you must not..."

He heard nothing of Bessie's warning, his stride quickening as he found his way inside.

A fat, pompous man sat in the office, smoking a pipe that reeked of poor tobacco. His face waxed at the sight of the tall, broad-shouldered man inside his factory.

"What is the meaning of this?"

"Master William," Bessie whimpered from behind him. "This is not Mr. Smith."

"Who are you?" William growled. "Where is Mr. Smith?"

The chunky man struggled to rise from his chair, bursting a button on his vest in the process.

"I am Regis Wallopher!" he barked, his cheeks crimson with anger. "You have no right to enter my establishment."

"I will burn your establishment to the ground, with you inside, if you do not give me the address to your day manager," William growled, drawing closer to Regis Wallopher. The man drew back, three of his chins quivering.

"I-I-I…" he sputtered.

"I will not ask again," William insisted. "Give me his address now or so help me God…"

"He lives in Bromley!" Regis squeaked. "I'll fetch the directions."

Glowering, William awaited his handwritten direction, his eyes narrowing to slits.

"I would prefer not to return here," he snapped, looking about the torrid conditions in which Bessie had worked with Sarah. "Please do not make me."

With shaking hands, Regis Wallopher handed the page, scrawled with directions, to the incensed young man and immediately drew back as if anticipating an assault.

"You ought to be ashamed of yourself," William muttered, storming from the office, Bessie in tow.

"Master William, he'll have my job," Bessie whispered, a small cough falling from her lips in the aftermath of her declaration. William paused and gazed at her, sadness overcoming him.

"You should never have been working here in the first place," he announced furiously. "It's good riddance to bad rubbish, I say."

Bessie crushed her lips together and said nothing, following him through the streets of the East End, darkness enshrouding them as they ventured further into the city limits. William paused several times to get his bearings, reading Wallopher's map and reorienting himself until they turned down a quiet row. Only the moon prevailed here, no street lamps to guide their way but William permitted his intuition to guide him until an hour later he and Bessie stood before a small, unkempt house.

"Is this it?" Bessie murmured, speaking for the first time in almost half an hour, her face constricting with worry. A scream and crash from inside the house answered her query, the pair rushed toward the front door without considering the consequences.

William pushed through the front door, his heart racing as he crashed through the doorway. To his left, Sarah lay pinned beneath the sinewy frame of an ugly-faced man as she struggled. William's hand took the scruff of his neck, yanking Mr. Smith from her body to throw him back against the wall. The man landed with a thud, his bones cracking with the impact.

"W-Will?!" Sarah gasped in shock. William fixed his attention on Mr. Smith, daring the smaller man to come for him.

"Who are you? Get out of my house!" Mr. Smith screamed, enraged and in pain. He struggled to his feet but did not venture closer, perhaps reading the ire in William's face with clarity.

"William, you're alive!" Sarah sobbed, dumbfounded as Bessie appeared tentatively behind him. "Bessie?"

"Be gone or I shall call a constable!" Mr. Smith howled.

"Very well," William agreed, extending his hand for Sarah to take. "We will leave."

"You cannot take her!" the manager roared. "She is my intended!"

Relief washed through William as he realised that their union had not been legalised.

"Impossible," he snarled. "She is my family and I have not agreed to this union."

"She has no family!"

"She does," William insisted, helping Sarah to her feet. "Whatever contract you have coerced from Miss Joyce does not apply. She is coming with me."

He glared furiously at Mr. Smith, and the man was far too cowardly to fight.

"Take her then!" Mr. Smith whined. "She's spoilt goods anyhow."

William untangled his hand from Sarah's, clenching his fist to punch the snivelling man directly on the nose. Blood spurted forth and Mr. Smith began to cry but William did not waste a moment relishing in his handiwork. He was grateful that his fist had finally found a proper target after the week he had endured.

"Come along," he ordered the women, reclaiming Sarah's hand and marching her and Bessie from the house. The servant rushed after them and the trio hurried into the night, leaving Mr. Smith and his stone house prison in the darkness where they belonged.

CHAPTER 12

Sarah's stupefaction did not lessen as William half carried her through the cobblestone streets of London. Bessie spoke words that she did not hear, her azure eyes fixated on the ghost at her side.

How can this be? Have I died and gone to Heaven?

She barely noticed the finer avenues until she was led through a side entrance and up the stairs, flanked by Bessie and the man she had believed dead for several years.

It was not until they were securely in a room, the door locked, and Sarah sat upon a brass bed did she understand that this was no dream at all.

"You're truly here!" she muttered, shaking her head as she studied the face she had dreamt of every night. "How can this be?"

William crouched before her, gently placing his hands on her knees as Bessie turned away, fussing about the basin as she avoided watching the reunited pair.

"I was lost at sea for a time," he explained, taking her hand, his eyes wide with marvel as they raked over her face. "Forgive me for not having been here, Sarah. You must know I thought of you every day."

He glanced over his shoulder at Bessie, his cheeks tinging pink as he heard his own confessions. "I tried to imagine what you would look like now but you…"

He inhaled deeply, stopping him speaking for a moment.

"You've become more lovely than I ever envisioned."

Warmth and joy crept into Sarah's veins, the reality of her situation overcoming her in a wave so intense, she could not stop herself from what she next did. Her arms encircled William's neck and she drew him close, placing her lips upon him to taste the credulity of her position. His mouth was warm, real, present.

Abruptly, she drew back, a hand flying to her lips in dismay.

"Oh," she whispered. "Forgive me, Will."

Humiliated, she turned away, shaking her head.

"I-I've thought of you so often and regretted that you never truly knew how I felt about you."

Tears sprang into her eyes, and she rose to pace the room. Bessie did her best to hide herself, but it was clear the older woman was listening intently to the interaction between the pair, a small smile touching her lips.

"Is it sinful that I've grown to love you as more than a brother?" she breathed, her cheeks afire. She wrapped her arms around her body and kept her back to him, unsure of how he would react to such a confession.

She felt him near but did not turn, her embarrassment too overpowering.

I will always be that impulsive girl from the hull of the ship, she thought, anguished. *And now I've ruined our relationship with my flapping mouth.*

A gentle hand turned her around, William's kindly grey eyes fastened on her face.

"My love for you has no title or name," he told her huskily. "Our love was not borne from parentage or ancestry. Our bond did not grow from knowing a single womb or kinship, Sarah."

His words sent shivers through her, his earnestness dispelling her concerns.

"Every night, I reread your letters, memorising every word. I could read them back to you from my mind alone," he murmured, drawing her closer. "Brother, guardian, friend… husband…I am your family, Sarah, however you choose to have me."

The tears that had filled her eyes fell, one by one as William wiped them away.

"I'll never leave you again," he vowed, kissing the top of her head and embracing her tightly. "You have my word."

Sarah dropped her head against his chest, the easy thump of his heart lulling her into a sense of ease she had not known in years. Her prayers had been answered. By some miracle of God, William had been returned to her, their lives intertwined again as fate had intended.

"Your father would be so pleased to see this," Bessie sniffed, pulling the pair apart. Bashfully, they eyed her nodding solemnly.

"I imagine that Mr. Tavers sensed your love for one another," the servant told them softly. "He was not a man of many words but his affections for you both were tangible."

William smiled at the woman.

"And for you, Bessie," he said quietly. "I know that my father held a special place in his heart for you."

Bessie smiled, her back straightening at the thought that Joseph Tavers may have cared for her as more than merely his housekeeper.

"What will we do now?" Sarah asked, looking about the chamber. "Surely you haven't enough money to stay here much longer, and I have no doubt that our jobs at the mill have been rescinded."

Bessie grimaced but William was unconcerned. William shook his head and took her hands again.

"Money is not a cause for fretting, my dear," he promised confidently. "My father, wealthy as he were, instilled that in me from a young age. We will make do with what we have."

Sarah glanced at Bessie.

"We've done so thus far," she agreed.

"Provided we have one another, we will overcome life's hardships. It is how Joseph Tavers raised us both, was it not?"

"And me?" Bessie squeaked. "What will become of me?"

William glanced at her, a rueful grin touching his lips.

"If you are not family, Bessie, then I don't know the meaning of the word."

Relief washed over her face, and she fell into a nearby chair as though her legs would no longer hold her. William and Sarah stared into one another's eyes again, savouring the current surging between them.

He is correct. All will be overcome, as long as we are together.

EPILOGUE

The tinkle of piano keys spilt through the house as little fingers danced across the ivory.

"Well done, May." Sarah laughed lightly when the child finished her piece. "You've come a long way since our last lesson."

May smiled proudly at her teacher and nodded assertively.

"I have been driving my mother mad with all my practice," she replied, her bright eyes unblinking. Sarah smothered a laugh. "I swear she curses the day she agreed to allow me to have lessons."

"I'm sure that's hardly the case."

"I don't much mind," May prattled on, sliding from the bench. "I intend to play for the Royal Opera House one day and I must practice every day to ensure that happens."

"I'm certain that if you continue to study as you have, that dream is certain to become a reality," Sarah replied honestly.

The front door opened, and William entered, pausing to see the pair at the piano.

"Oh, forgive the intrusion," William called, moving to back out of his home. "I did not realise you had lessons today, my darling."

"We've just finished, dearest," Sarah replied, waving him forward as May moved to leave. The little girl smiled at William, batting her long-lashed eyes coquettishly at him.

"I do hope that one day my husband speaks to me as kindly as you speak to Mrs. Tavers," May told him rather too honestly. "My father never speaks to my mother with such warmth."

She was gone before Sarah could react to such a dismal statement, but William found the words amusing.

"I daresay we're apt to sicken all of the neighbourhood if we continue to openly care for one another as we do."

"Their jealousy is of no concern to me," Sarah replied, rising to greet him with a soft kiss upon his cheek. He carried the smell of the sea with him, the scent of salt and fish permeating his clothes, but it did not bother Sarah now. It was indicative of a hard day's work. William was now a foreman on the docks where his father had once kept his cargo ships, but his feet never left the land, but to unload the boats on occasion.

"She did not pay again today," Sarah murmured worriedly. "I will speak with her father next week."

William removed his hat and coat, resting them near the door.

"The girl is a prodigy," he teased. "Surely she will pay her own way when she joins the theatre."

His nonchalance warmed Sarah's heart. Their lives were not as wealthy as they had been under Joseph's roof but with William's pay and her piano lessons, they had enough. A late payment or two would not force them into destitution.

"I received an offer today," William said, flopping unceremoniously into his favourite chair near the fire. "Double the pay."

Sarah's flaxen eyebrows rose, her pulse quickening but not with excitement.

"Doing what?" she asked, certain she knew the answer. It would not be the first time William had been presented with opportunities. The Tavers name still bore some weight and his experiences at sea had done well for his reputation.

"Scouting trade posts in the Caribbean."

Sarah balked, pressing her lips together as she studied her husband through her peripheral vision.

"Naturally, I refused," he added before she could permit herself to grow upset. Relief sank into her bones, but it was coupled with guilt.

"That is a fair sum they've offered you," she told him weakly.

"There is not a sum in the world they could offer which would take me from your side again," he replied as she slunk closer. Tentatively, she sat on his lap, placing her hands on his windblown cheeks.

"I know you made that promise to me two years ago," she murmured. "But I would not hold you to it if you felt the desire to go."

"The only desire I feel is here, with you."

A cry echoed through the house, turning both their heads toward the stairs. Bessie was descending, a wailing infant swaddled in her arms.

"Forgive the intrusion, Ma'am, Mr. Tavers," she said with a sigh, "but the bairn will not stop her crying."

Sarah rose to take the baby from Bessie's arms, but William moved faster, taking the child and holding it close to his body.

"There, there, little one," he cooed, his eyes shining with affection as he stared into the small, beautifully formed face before him. "There's no need for such theatrics."

Instantly, the baby calmed, a tiny fist raised toward her father's face.

"He certainly has a way with her," Bessie marvelled aloud, echoing Sarah's own thoughts. "He reminds me of how the first Mr. Tavers was, with him."

Sarah's heart swelled at the sight of father and child together, a hand reaching out to grasp Bessie's.

"Life truly does come full circle, does it not?" Sarah murmured, watching as William rocked his daughter back into slumber.

"Indeed," Bessie agreed. "This is why she is so aptly named."

Josephine cooed happily, her hand curling around William's dirty finger, blue eyes alight with comfort and love. She was her father's daughter and her grandfather's namesake. She would not know any of the suffering they had all endured to bring her this life.

We are all safe and protected, just as Joseph Tavers planned. May he rest in eternal peace knowing that his family is together and thriving...

~*~*~

Thank you so much for reading my story.

If you enjoyed reading this book may I suggest that you might also like to read my recent release 'Saving the Wretched Slum Girl' next which is available on Amazon for just £0.99 or free with Kindle Unlimited.

Click Here to Get Your Copy Today!

Sample of First Chapter

Seven-year-old Alice Smythe was small for her age, which in some ways was a bonus as it allowed her to work as a scavenger mule at the Langford Cotton Mill, in the East End of London. She and her mother had worked there together for the past six months, Alice having commenced her employment at the mill the day after her seventh birthday.

They toiled from dawn till dusk often not seeing the outside light during the day at all. She listened intently to the clacking of the machinery as it moved back and forth, the spindle catching the yarn at the top and winding it up, as if it were a spinning top she had seen once at the travelling fair.

Alice needed to be careful when she scrambled underneath, she knew the work was dangerous—her mother had reminded her many times—but her family needed the money to survive. The loud deafening sound of the busy machinery no longer hurt her ears as it had in her first few months, her mother had told her to push some cotton fluff in them to dull the noise and she wore a remnant of cloth across her mouth to keep the loose threads and cotton dust from clogging up her throat and lungs.

Her mother suffered from a nasty cough, brought on by years of working in the hot, humid conditions that were needed in a cotton mill. She would hear her in the middle of the night getting up gasping for air, drinking to try and relieve the spasms, but nothing seemed to help. Her cough was getting much worse but still she needed to work else they would end up in the workhouse and that would be dishonourable beyond words. No one ever wanted to end up there, it would be a disgrace.

As quick as a mouse, she darted under the dangerous mechanical movement, keeping her head low, almost touching the filthy wooden floor as she gathered up the loose cotton balls that had fallen from the equipment. Her small nimble fingers tucked them into the pocket of the dark apron that her mother had placed around her waist just this morning. Dashing forward before the machine could complete another turn, Alice darted out on the other side— she was safe this time.

Even at the young age of seven, Alice knew that there was a heavy risk around the machines. Her mother would warn her several times a day to be careful about watching her head and keeping her wits about her at all times. While she didn't enjoy the task she had been given, Alice knew that her family badly needed the extra money now that her father wasn't able to work. It was up to Alice and her mother, Mary to find the necessary finances to support them. They were luckier than some, she was an only child, Alice couldn't imagine how hard it must be for families with several children.

Alice hurried around the machine, placing the loose cotton scraps into the storage barrel that would be taken away at the end of the day, dumping the oddments into the large vats of leftover fragments. Alice liked the way the soft cotton felt between her fingertips. Just the other day she had put some in her pocket and taken it home, keeping it under her pillow to touch in the cold dark nights. She would have been whipped by Master Turney, the foreman, if he had found out, but Alice hadn't been forced to empty her pockets that particular day, so no one knew and now she had something of her own that no one else knew about.

Not even her mother…

"Alice! Stop daydreaming. The cotton isn't going to pick itself up!"

Her mother's voice cut through her thoughts and Alice darted under the machine once more, gathering up the cotton. A few strands of fine blonde hair clung to Alice's moist neck as she quickly finished her task. Her mother made her wear a dark brown mop cap so that her hair wouldn't get trapped in the constantly moving machinery above her head, telling her daughter that she had seen it happen once, that a little girl had been scalped before they could stop the machines. All of Alice's clothes were either brown or black in colour, her mother insisted that she wear dark clothing. After all, you couldn't see the dirt if it was the same colour as the material, she would say.

"Smythe!"

Alice cringed at the sound of Master Turney's shrill voice, scurrying out of his path as he bared down on her mother.

Having worked at the Langford Cotton Mill for most of her life, her mother didn't even flinch at the man's putrid breath hovering over her. "Yes, Master Turney?" she answered plainly.

He pointed at Alice, who was peeking out from behind one of the machines. "Why isn't your gel sweeping the floor like she is paid to do?" the man growled angrily.

"I will have her do it straightaway, Master Turney," her mother replied. Alice didn't waste any time finding the broom. Hurrying as far away as possible from the conversation, she set to sweeping up the dust and cotton fragments too small to be picked up. She didn't like Master Turney and very few workers at the factory did. He was a nasty vicious bully, who wouldn't think twice about using his fists to get what he wanted.

Her small body moved the broom furiously over the grimy floor, causing a small cloud of dust to rise which tickled her nose through her face covering, but she managed not to sneeze. In the near distance, she saw a familiar face, nine-year-old John Cartwright, walking through the hallway. It was unbelievable that he was back at work so soon after his terrible accident.

He was one of the piecers, a job known to be very dangerous, and John had proved the point. He had not been in work for the past few days. Alice remembered back to the day when John had been hurt, she had never seen so much blood before in her young life and, despite the fact that her mother had tried to shield her from it, Alice had still seen enough of the carnage to scare her for a lifetime.

Poor John had got his hand caught trying to repair the broken threads, he had foolishly tried to grab his cap that had been dislodged because he was growing too tall.

"What's he doin' here, he canna work like that?" the foreman shouted above the roar of the machines. "Look at that bandage, there's still blood seeping through."

"I promise ye he can still work, just as well. He's a strong lad. Put him on moving the barrels or helping with sweeping the floors. Please, I beg of ye," his mother, Myrtle pleaded. She was a thin scraggy woman and most folks in the factory knew that John and Myrtle depended on the work to support his younger siblings. His father had passed just five months ago from the same cough that Alice's poor mother was displaying.

Alice swallowed as her eyes trailed towards the bandage, gasping when she realised that it was evident that two of his fingers were not where they should be.

Shaking his head, Turney relented, sending John to the docking area where the cotton came in to be sent to the looms, yelling for the trembling woman to get back to her work too. The rest of the day passed by slowly and without incident and by the time the sun was starting to fade through the filth ingrained windows, Alice's hands were covered in fresh bulging blisters from holding the broom far too tightly.

Passing down the last aisle, she swept the dust away from the pathways between the looms. Just as she was finishing up, she heard raised voices and crept a little closer to the sound.

"I don't care what you were doing! You weren't here, Nicholas! That is all that matters. I want you here and in *my* bed at night."

"Now, you listen to me, I had business to attend to, Catherine. You couldn't possibly understand what I was doing."

Alice took a quick peek in the direction the voices were coming from, her eyes widening, when she saw the owner of the Mill, Mr Nicholas Langford, standing close by, next to his wife, Catherine Langford. Mr Langford was dressed in a fine dark charcoal grey suit, the shiny golden chain of a pocket watch swaying across the front of his rather portly stomach that was covered by colourful floral waistcoat. Catherine Langford was dressed in a gown that was perhaps the loveliest that Alice had ever seen, having a deep crimson colour with pretty cream coloured lacework at the neck and cuffs. Alice wondered if the material felt as soft and smooth as it looked.

She would never attempt to touch the fabric, however, that would never do, it would be cause for instant dismissal. She could see that Catherine Langford was annoyed as she glared angrily at her husband. Alice had seen that stance many times before. It was the same one that her mother liked to use when Alice was misbehaving. She was intrigued to know what was going on and she couldn't help but stand stock still and gawp as the couple continued to argue.

"Oh, Nicholas, I'm well aware of what you were doing," Catherine Langford said, her hands flying about wildly. "You were with that hussy again, weren't you?"

Mr Langford stepped forward, hands raised as he tried to placate his angry wife. "Come, come, you don't know what you are talking about."

Catherine Langford laughed audibly and there was a bitterness to the high-pitched sound. "Oh, Nicholas, I am not as naïve as you may think. I know you have a mistress and have done for some time." Alice gasped at the woman's strange words. She knew she shouldn't continue to listen to another's private conversation, but she simply couldn't help herself. Catherine Langford continued speaking, her voice a little lower now. "That is not why I sought you out though. Our son, Matthew, is due to return from school for the summer break. I expect he will be going back at the start of the autumn term."

"Mm-hm," Nicholas acknowledged, clearing his throat. "I'm not sure that is a good idea. I suggest he comes to work in the mill so he can come to understand some of what he is destined to inherit. It's about time he learnt the family trade. That's how I learnt the goings on of this establishment—from my father, not by spending money on an expensive education."

"I understand, but he will still be returning to school to finish his education. I insist," Mrs Langford stated plainly, pushing her index finger into the man's chest to prove her point. "He's destined for greatness. He may not have a title, but that does not matter in this time of vast economic growth."

"As you well know, my darling," the man replied, a cruel sneer spreading across his face. "This is our livelihood. It is what pays for your fancy gowns and afternoon teas with those simpering women you call your friends. Of course, he will finish the necessary education but then he is expected to learn how to run this factory. Too much of a fancy education isn't going to help without the practical experience to help him get on in life."

Catherine Langford didn't look as if she was about to back down and Alice waited to see what the man would do next. "As long as you allow him to complete his studies, I will be satisfied," she said placing her hands firmly on her hips. "But you are not to renege on your word."

"S'cuse me, Mr Langford. We need to talk about them workers and which ones ain't pulling their weight and what we need to do about 'em?"

The couple turned as Master Turney approached them, causing Alice to shrink back into the shadows, her young mind attempting to sort out the conversation she had just overheard. So, the owner had a son, one that she was not aware of. What good fortune he had, never needing to work in this grimy, dirt-laden mill but going to school to learn to read and write, something she had always dreamt of doing.

Sighing with frustration, she quickly finished her work before making her way back to her mother. "Ready, my darling gel?" her mother asked trying to smother a cough, tightening the scarf around her head and handing Alice her coat. "There is a cold wind out there. We wouldn't want to catch our deaths, so button up and come along with me," she continued holding out her hand for Alice to take.

Alice donned her coat and thin woollen scarf before making their way down the stone steps with the other workers, their workday finally at an end. Alice stayed close to her mother as they exited the mill, grasping her hand lightly. The lamp lighters were already out, lighting the smoggy streets, allowing them a dull glow with which to find their way home. By the time they got back, Alice's nose was red and streaming from the cold.

Her father eagerly awaited them inside, leaning heavily on his crutch as they entered in a flurry. "There you are," he cried as Alice shrugged out of her coat. "I have made us some dinner."

Her mother gave him a grateful smile, knowing that there was little food to be had and it would have been difficult to cook something nourishing for them all. "That was kind of you, Frank. I'm sorry we are late."

Alice gave her father a tight hug, careful not to topple him over. "Thank you, Papa."

"Oh, my darling gel. You don't have to thank me for anything," he said, returning her embrace.

Alice gazed up at him and saw the sadness in his eyes as he looked down at her. Her father had also once worked in the mill. However, an inexperienced hand had incorrectly stacked some barrels, causing them to escape their confines, crushing his leg beyond repair. With his badly deformed leg and the crutch he required to get around, no mill was willing to offer him work—to them he was as good as useless.

It didn't matter to Alice, though, he was still her Papa and she loved him more than anybody else in the world, apart from her Mama of course, who she loved equally.

"Come, Alice," her mother said pulling her towards the enamel washbasin. "Let's get cleaned up."

Alice dutifully did as her mother asked, forcing her hands into the frigid water.

Her stomach grumbled, reminding her of how hungry she was, although there would be barely enough food, being that the family had to survive on the pittance that she and her mother earned. Times may be hard in the Smythe household, but Alice knew there was always plenty of love to go around.

~*~*~

This wonderful Victorian Romance story — 'Saving the Wretched Slum Girl' — is available on Amazon for just £0.99 or *FREE* with Kindle Unlimited simply by clicking on the link below.

[Click Here to Get Your Copy of 'Saving the Wretched Slum Girl' - Today!](#)

A NOTE FROM THE AUTHOR

Dear Reader,

Thank you so much for choosing and reading my story — I sincerely hope it lived up to your expectations and that you enjoyed it as much as I loved writing about the Victorian era.

This age was a time of great industrial expansion with new inventions and advancements.

However, it is true to say that there was a distinct disparity amongst the population at that time — one that I like to emphasise, allowing the characters in my stories to have the chance to grow and change their lives for the better.

Best Wishes
Ella Cornish

∽

Newsletter

If you love reading Victorian Romance stories…

Simply sign up here and get your FREE copy of The Orphan's Despair

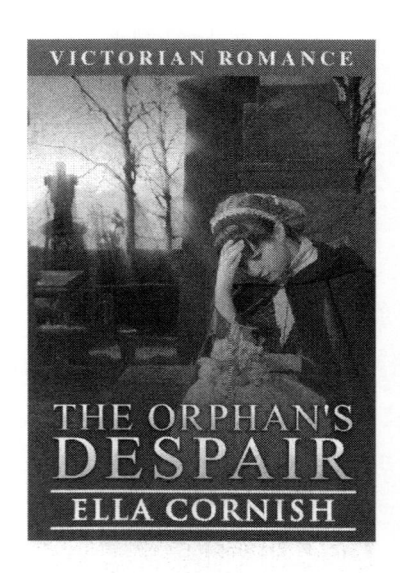

Click Here to Download Your Copy - Today!

∽

More Stories from Ella!

If you enjoyed reading this story you can find more great reads from Ella on Amazon...

Click Here for More Stories from Ella Cornish

∽

Contact Me

If you'd simply like to drop us a line you can contact us at **ellacornishauthor@gmail.com**

You can also connect with me on my Facebook Page **https://www.facebook.com/ellacornishauthor/**

I will always let you know about new releases on my Facebook page, so it is worth liking that if you get the chance.

LIKE Ella's Facebook Page *__HERE__*

I welcome your thoughts and would love to hear from you!

Printed in Great Britain
by Amazon